CARRYING THE BODY

A NOVEL

Dawn Raffel

SCRIBNER

New York   London   Toronto   Sydney   Singapore

SCRIBNER
1230 Avenue of the Americas
New York, NY 10020

SCRIBNER and design are trademarks of
Macmillan Library Reference USA, Inc., used under license
by Simon & Schuster, the publisher of this work.

For information about special discounts for bulk purchases,
please contact Simon & Schuster Special Sales:
1-800-456-6798 or business@simonandschuster.com

Text set in Aldine

Manufactured in the United States of America

1   3   5   7   9   10   8   6   4   2

Library of Congress Cataloging-in-Publication Data
Raffel, Dawn
Carrying the body : a novel / Dawn Raffel.
p.   cm.
1. Problem families—Fiction. I. Title.
PS3568.A372   C37   2002
813'.54—dc21   2002066864

ISBN 13: 978-1-4165-7510-8   ISBN 10: 1-4165-7510-3

For Mike
and for our sons, Brendan and Sean Harry

Acknowledgments

I would like to acknowledge my father, Mark Raffel, who championed this work from its inception—sometimes driving more than one hundred miles to hear me read—but did not live to see its publication. Thanks are due to so many people; first and foremost, it must be said that every writer should be blessed with an editor as fine as Rachel Sussman at Scribner. I am grateful to Gordon Lish, Patricia Volk, and Gail Galloway Adams. The editors of the literary magazines who supported this book as it progressed include Diane Williams, Christine Schutt, Ben Marcus, Bradford Morrow, Deron Bauman, Michael Koch, Michael Neff, David McLendon, and Gary Lutz. I also want to thank Nan Graham, Jennifer Lyons, Hamza Walker and the Renaissance Society at the University of Chicago, John Searles, Tracy Young, Jennifer Belle, Elizabeth Tippens, and Amy Gross. My phenomenal boss, Oprah Winfrey, nurtures what is best in those whose lives she touches, and I'm grateful to be among them. Finally and always, my family—especially, but not solely, my mother, Francine; Cherie, Stuart, Lee, David, Joan, and Maureen—have given me more than I can express.

Portions of *Carrying the Body* have been previously published as follows:

"Late" (as "The Train Had Been Late") in *Epoch*

"Blood of the Morning" (as "Freight") in *Story Quarterly*

"Once, Twice, Three Times" on Failbetter.com

"A Bedtime Tale" (as "Is Anybody Listening?") in *Conjunctions,* reprinted on Web del Sol and in the anthology *Wild Women* (Carroll & Graf)

"Squeal" in *Noon*

"Must I Tell You Again?" on Elimae.com

"Sweet" on 5 Trope and, in slightly different form, in *Micro Fictions* (Norton)

"Abandon" on Web del Sol, Editor's Picks

"The Aunt Sweeps" and "The Aunt's Dream" in *Arts & Letters*

"Grooming" in *Noon* and on Elimae.com

"Where are you?" he said.

−Genesis 3:9

Part One

THE BRIDE

Late

THE CHILD HAD a rash across the chest, a fearsome swath of color—infection, the aunt thought, bred of the child. Mold on dough. Blood mold. Why, look at the child, just look at the child!—dripping, it seemed, the irises fluid—red in the nose, the cheeks, pale belly as if risen; and there in an indolent fist, a bulbous, sucked-on toy in the likeness of some sort of life-form.

"What, this?" said the mother. "This?" It was only the weather, the mother said, the heat, this rash.

The sight of her, the aunt thought: wan unironed sister in the light. The hand a fleshy visor. Useless. To have traveled like this, with the heat and with the child, in the festering light, no bags but bags, the aunt observed, brown paper gone to pulp, as if juice had leaked or milk had leaked or sodden, fungal diapers; and clothes spilling over the tops of the bags, such clothes you could scarcely imagine, or not quite imagine, slack-hemmed, rayon, secondhand, the aunt supposed, with rounds of stain below the arms, a bra strap dingy as unrinsed teeth. "I have never . . ." the aunt said. "Never mind."

The platform was empty.

The train had been late.

The child lacked a shirt. "Up," he said. He looked at her: aunt, tall stranger, relation. There he stood with bare, afflicted chest—arms held out, toy held out, offered to her, beseeching her, and yet, the aunt thought, there was something familial and hard about the brow.

"Here," she said. "I'll lend a hand." She took a bag. Her dress began to dampen. "Shall we?" she said. "Shall we hasten?" she said, and her sister—a touch, a breast, a way of moving, Mama to the child, Elise her name—said yes.

They walked. The child toddled. The tracks were beside them. "James," said the mother, Elise, for the child had come into possession of things—a pebble, twig, a splinter. "Jim," she said. A berry. "Baby," she called him. Poison? "Drink?" she said, and lifted him (one-armed, muscled, the aunt saw) squalling to a hip. The wonder the toy not lost.

It was in the mother's mouth.

It was in the child's hand.

"There, in there," the mother said.

"What in where?" the aunt said.

"The juice," the mother said. "In that sack. Yes, I think so. Would you be so good?"

The aunt made a motion and soiled herself. The child yelped. The bag the aunt held had no bottom. The child dragged fingers across broken skin.

The mother ("Mama!" "Elise!") with the child ("James," she said, her voice a scratch) and with a bag herself (still holding things) and with, of course, the toy, and with what looked to the aunt to be considerable effort, crouched. "Lord," said the mother. "Lord on high." She had her hair in her face, and her clothes were in the road, and the road rather presently was sifted through her fingers. Earth, a sock, a sock—not hers, this last, she said—a sopping wrapper, used. "Don't," she said, "touch that." And turning to the aunt, to her sister, "Juice," she said, as if saying, the aunt thought, "Don't just watch."

The aunt, of course, watched. And more than that, she was thinking: What of her dress, she thought, her scarf, her carefully thought-out ensemble? And what of the ruined bag? It was still in her hands; and still on the tip of her tongue, this: "Elise," she said (she said this much), "stand up, leave it. Think about him. Will you think about him?"

The mother sniffed a garment.

"Child," the aunt said. "You have not seen him. He is not right," and to the child: "Soon," she said. "Why, as soon as we get there, you're to have wholesome milk."

The place was not the aunt's. Suppose, for the sake of discussion, the place was the father's. (Not of the child, no, but of the aunt; the father of the aunt, and of the mother of the child, of course, of Elise.) The place was not kept up. That it was not kept up is not open to question. Try, the aunt thought, try and be of help, try and be of service, try and be a neighborly, a daughterly daughter, and what, the aunt thought, what with whatever, what without thanks, why, one got what? Dirt, the aunt thought, that was what: the cellophane nibbled in the pantry, crumbs, rice, a yeasty smear, the place as if in motion. Oh, such birth! Here the aunt had grown, slow inch upon inch as if awaiting an occasion to rise to; here Elise had grown, turned in on herself. The father's bones rose out of the body. Veins, hairs, moles—the sickened mass of him! The chair in an unbudgeable condition of recline.

Just who, the aunt said, entering, did she, Elise, suppose it was that she, the aunt, looked like? Had she done her part? Was she the father's mother? "After all," the aunt said.

There was spittle in an ashtray.

The child appeared to be looking at the aunt with what appeared to the aunt to be a fever in the eyes.

Elise crossed the threshold. "Pop," she said. "Yes?" she said, with arms full, always with arms full, exertion in the mouth, in the angle of the jaw, and in the ungroomed frizz about the forehead and nape.

The skin, the aunt thought, was looking worse.

"Girls?" said a voice. It was failing and gruff. "Girls? Girls?"

The aunt dabbed a temple, and gently, with a certain decorum, her chest, the tissue at the bosom pinkly crushed. She tasted salt—the lips so damaged! (Nothing, the aunt had said, might cross them.) "My," she said.

"Me," said the child, James, Jim, Baby, Yoo-hoo, whichever one it was. "Me, me, me."

Feet to the floorboards. "You," said the mother. "Put that down," and to the aunt, who had (rather deftly, the aunt thought) produced dried milk, said, "You are not the mother. No sirree."

The child said, "I see you."

The aunt changed clothes in a dank space smelling of mothballs. Collars at attention awaited a neck. Dear, departed woman: Mother of the aunt and of the mother of the child and of her own demise—swift passage, hers. No tumor-ragged body or bloated cheek, reformed and by-passed heart. She'd left them all: the reptile purses, topcoats of fur, things hoarded and abandoned. Nothing was light, nothing was lightweight, winterweight the whole of it, as if, the aunt thought, there had been no thought of a season such as this, no thought of an eventual spring.

She, the aunt, zipped, was bursting at the seams.

The mother of the child did not change.

The child continued to want for a shirt.

The aunt spoke up, but in such a way so as not to be heard, she thought, and halfway hoped: The child's growth was stunted, the health of the child ignored. "Neglected," she said. "Blatant," she said.

Jellied, the child rolled bread, chewed open-mouthed.

At the foot of the chair was the toy.

The toy had eyes.

"Pop," said the mother, Elise. "This is my son."

A sound arose in the father's throat. "The shade," he said. "Will you pull it?" he said (there was no shade), and "This, this—this is what I want. This is what I need from the pantry." Say it was these: sweets, rags, a cigarette. He used the aunt's name. "Auntie?" he said. "Is it a boy, did you say?"

The aunt gave the mother of the child a well-worn look.

Exposed, the child covered and uncovered and re-covered his face. He yanked at the mother. "Mama," he said. "Mama!"

"Oh," said the mother. "Peekaboo."

"Like this for this?" the aunt said. "Did you come for this? Was this what you came for? Hours, after all," the aunt said, "on the train." (Days, perhaps, for all she knew—wherever it was they had come from escaped her—rank stops, the clothes left to scatter.) "And," the aunt said, "need I add, after year after year of no word?"

"Pop," said the mother, addressing the chair, herself in shabby clothing, the house gauzed in heat, the hoarded effects of the dead: Oh, come to me.

"And," the aunt said, "he, yes, our mutual father asleep in the chair, insensible," the aunt said. "Almost. Do you recognize him?" Discolored, sickly sleeper—she had taken care, had made herself careworn.

"Pop," said the mother. "Pop," as if *she* were the child—which, of course, she was. She had the clothes on her back. No trinket of Mother, nothing of Father. Nothing for sale or show, save him, the boy, disfathered heir, who (needn't she add it?) was bright. Or, at the least, not addled or dim. "I do not want much," she said.

The aunt thought: money; the aunt thought: shelter; the aunt thought: doctor; the aunt thought: maybe decent clothes, respect for the elders (of which she was one), and someone to see to the boy.

The mother faced men's shoes. "Do you remember?" the mother said, "how Mother would dress us to show us off? The way she used to dress us?—such fine things." For it was all of it shared: bow, ring, earrings, the freckles on the arms. And then, of course, the petticoats, Elise's often fallen, even with Mother's intervention, at a hem.

The father, in his sleep, was heard to cough. He dreamed of what? The aunt did not dream, not ever, even

9

once, or else did not recall it. Mornings with the taste of the breath in her mouth, her thinning hair wound tight.

"Don't you remember?" the mother said.

The father seemed to fret.

"No," the aunt said. "No, you don't. Oh no, you don't." Said, "Don't even try it on me at all."

The child coughed up blood. This was in the night, in the dark of the house, in a room that went unused. It was midnight, give or take. The mother arose. The aunt, aroused, could not recall exactly where she was. She could not place herself—how old was she now and what did she look like?

The mother of the child—her sister, Elise—appeared to her. Ah, the aunt thought (said it to herself—"Ah"). Look at her, the aunt thought, so full of maternal disregard.

"Juice," said the mother.

The child cried. His fists were bloody things. His fists were at his face and at his bloody, scabby chest.

"There," said the mother.

"I do not live here," the aunt said.

A racket in the kitchen: a flick of a light, and leggy dispersal—spiders, rodents, whatnot. The patter of feet.

"The diaper," the aunt said, in spite of herself.

"Juice," said the mother. "There, there."

There was no juice.

Tonic in a bottle, the child's voice swelling, the aunt in

an inherited nightgown, inheritable robe—this touched her flesh—all cuffs and straining belt: "Did you come here for this?" the aunt's voice losing itself in the aunt's marred hand. There was age in the hand: cool, dry, boned, the fingers someone else's. "For this?" she said. "This? What good are you doing?"

The child shrieked.

"Please," said the mother. "Help me, please. Where did it get to? Where did it go? Where is it—Baby's doll?"

The aunt in darkness saw it, or thought, at least, she saw it: The father of the aunt and of the mother of the child opened his eyes and closed his eyes. "Papa," she said, on her way past the chair. She touched her breast. She entered a hallway.

The mother, Elise, holding the child—James, Jim, Baby, blistering offspring, bottled at last, asleep at last, at last in Mother's arms and presumed to be dreaming: Such rich milk! Oh, wheel of my sleep!—knelt down by the father's chair. "See?" she said. "Father?"

The body of the father made a noise. His chest rose and shook. It rose and it shook.

The mother of the child swayed with the child. "Father," she said. "Oh, Father," she said, and the aunt in darkness heard it.

Gin

"WHERE IS IT?" the aunt said. The hall light was off.
She was guiding herself with her hand along a surface. This
would leave a mark, she thought, likely as not. The touch
was rough. "Papa?" she said.

A slight misstep, not a person in the kitchen, save, of
course, herself, she thought. Better the lightlessness, perhaps, what with the spillage, what with dirt, what with
whatever went unwashed. She found what she sought here.
Easy as pouring.

The darkness was active.

Something escaped her.

The bed she desired to sleep in was where?

She had covered the bottle (how many fingers?), wiped
her chin.

"Papa?" she said.

"Who is it?" she said.

"Listen," she said.

"Fine," she said. "Defy me, then." Her hand moved to suffocate a cry in the mouth. Under her foot, a stone or twig or bit of glass, or some small thing the child had dropped, hurt.

A room opened up to her. The air seemed to blow. She felt the hair fall to her own flawed neck: a clip released.

There was, at the window, the slightest perceptible tremor, she thought. She felt it, the moment, the awful little shudder: a breath before the terrible racket arose.

Blood of the Morning

THE WHISTLE MIGHT have entered her sleep, perhaps—the train's report: all mineral and animal, and men
of fit throat, arrangers of cargo, with steam at the lips. She
knew these men by taste. Sweet and distant, she knew
these men in marrow or by iron intervention, in vessels in
the vessel of herself. Oh, blood of the morning, angel of
breath! A whiff of the heat by which, on occasion, she
chose to believe, on incomplete, compliant faith, she had
been, in a moment of excess, borne. She was Father in the
cartilage, the turn of the nose. The scent, though, the
smell of her, skin, hair, scalp, smoke, in which she had
grown, through which she breathed—it was Mother.
Unfortunate chin—from whom? Which bold, inventing
ancestor or penetrating lover, invented of a night? Awake
and not: hale journeyers! She'd known them by admis-

sion. Look, they are wearers of cloth, and with a permeating sweat, and with a fluid in the hand: hot drinks in cups, such darkly acrid stimulants. Acquired from where? Impermanent, uninventoried place—to this she rose. See her rising, the body conforming to what has been lost, been given up or been, in instinct, offered up, to all that has been lost in it, a jewel in the lobe, a girl among the girls and disinherited ideas of girls she has been. Defier, by inattention, of Mother, dead these years: the bloody wrist, the kiss half-formed in death—a girl and still a girl and not a girl at a window, nightdress loose. She is moving apace. Breasted, pierced and swabbed. A rumble in the belly. Carrier. A child did quit her womb. Boy blue! Cold-fingered one, defector of sheets, of walls. The mouth has been opened, the child made to bleat. The milk is spilt— imbibe it. Come interrupt the breast. He'd slept in her, did sleep in her bed still, unstill, pinked up at a nostril, the will of the lungs, of air and of its unrecorded passages, in, out, in the house of her father, a room in which someone dear had died. This room was hers, had once been hers. The floor of it was scraped. There was a lamp unlit, in the form of a lady, the shade a lacy skirt. The face of it was breakable. The child, of course, had continued to gain. He was chubby in the leg and doubled in the fist, a duly-rounded, maiden-cheeked, incontinent, disfathered heir. The windows lived, amid the backtracked echo and shadow of motion: Here is the twig, the seed, the heat.

The child had a fever. The child had a rash. She had felt it in the dark, a tender abrasion, a friction on the surface of the skin. Don't touch! She stood at a window, too well touched, untouched, a rib, a rib, thwarted hoarder of increase, a bearer of ill-got fruit, of breath. She smelled the boy's smell, through the chemistry of self—flesh, bruise, evaporated fluid, all the flushing and emission of a body in perpetual and failed reform. As if to the window-light she spoke. "James," she said. "Jim," she said, "Baby," unburdening him. There was no quilt. It was humid as the night of his begetting, damp as the throated whisper in the ear: *Elise, Elise, Elise.* And had she not heeded? And had she not given and taken leave? Ungroomed, unberthed. The boy slept on. No father here save hers: he who was somewhere heard to cough—phlegmy, or was it dust? And was it Father? In which reentered corridor, or cornered place? Was there a walker, at this late hour, in the house? A person trapped and made to roam? Unquiet, the boy did sleep, in witnessed thrash, his hair (their hair) unruly, his brow (their brow) severe, the little nose's bridge a narrow one. The body is carbon, the breath is furred, and here in the house of her own hot, willed, injurious birth, the tread of her mother resides in a step. Go where? To Father, young again or unconceived? The bud is on the limb, the engine on the track—a tune is forced through tongue and groove: *Go forth, go forth, go forth.* This has happened before. "James," she said. "Come." She was a woman unmanned and moving to a bed. So many nights! Oh, wanderer! In dreams shall they find you. She touched the hot cheek. She kissed the sweet ear, and she lay half-held in the trembling quiet of the dark of a house passed by

Once, Twice,
Three Times

"MORNING," THE aunt said.

"Morning?" Elise said.

"Morning," the aunt said.

"More?" said the child. (Or was it "morn"? the aunt thought. Whichever it was—"more," "morn,"—sounded muffled, distorted, a hum to the aunt.)

"The child repeats," Elise said.

The child said, "Mama."

"You see?" Elise said.

"No," the aunt said. "Morning. I said 'morning.'"

Elise, who appeared to the aunt to be somehow engaged in appraising the place, said, "Is it, in fact? Is it morning again?" She raised herself, elbowed up only ever so slightly, damp at the breast, it seemed to the aunt, and fair at the neck, as if even the sun had not touched her. And yet the aunt knew better, did she not? The bedding had traveled.

"Sweet," Elise said. He, the child, seemed pressed to her, flush to her.

"I trust you slept," the aunt said. She licked her sore lips. She was, although certainly loath to admit it, thirsty again. "Is that blood on the sheet?"

"Sheet?" said the child.

"Blood?" said Elise. She opened her mouth and covered her mouth. She yawned. "Oh?" she said. "Oh, this?" she said. "It's old."

The child said, "Mama."

The aunt said, "'Aunt.' Say 'aunt.' Can you say 'aunt'?" The aunt stayed put in her place at the threshold. How could she help it? Such parched lips! She licked again, maybe biting a little.

Elise said, "Aunt."

The child scratched his rashy chest.

"Heavens," the aunt said, hand on hip. It was all of it old—unfixed, she saw—this too-warm room, all the objects of habit untended, rendered new in disuse. Neglect had remade things. She, the aunt, had done her best. Her level and utmost. But whom did she look like? Was this house hers? This house was not hers.

The window was shut.

There were smudges on the curtains. To bring the child, the aunt thought, to such a place as this, and in such a condition. Why, what with the upkeep, what with sheets! On the topic of which, "You say it's dried?" the aunt said. She saw the child's face, the way the cheek had been imprinted. "So I see," the aunt said. "You slept. I can see it. What with whatever. Racket or not. While I, on the other hand—"

"The light," Elise said.

"—not a wink," the aunt said. "What with all the commotion."

"Baby?" the mother, Elise said. "What?"

The child had moved to the edge of the bed. He was touching something fragile. Lace: skirt—or, more rightly, a lampshade fashioned as such, the lamp in the shape of a lady, there on the nightstand abutting the bed, her porcelain face serene and wrecked, no bulb.

"The lamp," Elise said. She looked to the aunt as if, the aunt thought, to accuse her of something. "When did it happen?"

"Broken," the aunt said.

"When?" Elise said.

"Mama?" the child said, reaching to touch it. "Doll?" he said. "Mine?"

Elise rolled over to stay the child. "This is not a doll," she said. "No toy," she said. "Not yours. Mother, remember, treasured this." She asked the aunt, "When?"

The child looked, to the aunt, ready to cry. "Doll?" he said.

"Why in the world did you come here?" the aunt said. "Why? For this?"

"Not this," Elise said. "No."

The child's mouth puckered. His face seemed disturbed.

Elise, it appeared to the aunt, was preparing to sigh. "Must you excite him?" she said to the aunt.

The aunt drew back.

Elise reached upward to touch a ragged hem.

"Milk?" said the aunt. She was serving something.

The table wobbled.

"No," said the mother, Elise. "No milk. It might well make him worse."

"Milk?" the aunt said. "Milk? Drink?"

The father of the aunt and of the mother of the child did not answer.

"Very well, then," the aunt said. "As you wish."

She poured herself a splash.

"Morning," the aunt said.

"Milk?" said the child. "Milk?"

He tugged at the cuff of the robe on the aunt.

The milk was dried.

"Morning," the aunt said. "Morning, I said."

"Yes," said the mother, Elise. "I heard you the first time. When did it break? And how, might I ask?"

"Might you?" the aunt said. "Where were *you*? All these years away from us, and after what you did to her." She touched the lamp's shade.

The child appeared to the aunt to be seeking something. "Doll?" he said.

"I haven't the slightest idea," the aunt said. "Don't ask me. Don't look at me."

He let out a guttural, almost, the aunt thought, animal sound, the child did.

The sheet was crushed.

Her lips were split, the aunt thought. No balm in the house, at least none that she knew of.

"Look," Elise said. She had opened the nightstand and had in her hand a delicate thing for the child to sniff. "Lilac," Elise said. "Or something or other. Mother's sachet."

There were, as a matter of possible record, a number of fine things still in the house:

1. Lace and porcelain lamp (broken)
2. Silk robe (frayed cuffs)
3. Dainty cameo ring (and one earring)
4. Assorted outerwear (fur and the like)
5. Lined purses (supposedly but not, necessarily, empty)
6. Silver gentleman's timepiece (slow)
7. Heavy cutlery (including the cake knife)
8. The ashtray
9. Sheets (all with excellent thread count)
10. Bed (iron headboard)
11. Slippers (peau de soie)

"More?" Elise said. "Tonic or something?"

Where, the aunt thought, had the child gone off to?

"Tonic?" Elise said. "Something to drink?"

The aunt said, "Milk."

"What of it?" Elise said.

The aunt said, "Soporific."

The child appeared from out of the pantry.

"Mama?" he said. He covered his face.

"What is it?" Elise said.

"Sopping," Elise said.

"Heavens," the aunt said. "Blood?"

★   ★   ★

"You never could pour without dripping," the aunt said. "Look at this. The way she excused you. Ruinous. The bed tray ruined too for her. The finish of it damaged."

"What finish?" Elise said, wiping, rather haphazardly, up.

"Father?" the aunt said. "Something refreshing?"

The father (the aunt could have surely attested) grunted.

The aunt smelled something heavily floral.

"Sweet?" said the father. "Sweet? Sweet?"

"No," said the aunt. "Not her," said the aunt. "I'm sorry to say it, Mother is dead."

The shade of the lamp, the lady's skirt, was stained, the aunt conceded (to herself)—as if by heat or by light or by damp—all three, the aunt thought: thoughtlessness.

"Fine," Elise said. "Wasn't it?"

The aunt looked up, unpleasantly startled. "What are you doing here?" she said.

The child appeared to have blood on his fingers.

"Look at him," the aunt said. "What kind of a mother?"

"No—" said the mother.

"No kind of mother," the aunt said. "That is what."

"No," said the mother. "Do not touch. Whatever you do," she said to the child, "no more."

One more somewhat fine thing:

12. Window curtains (gauze)

"Morning," the aunt said.

"Morning?" Elise said, holding the child's too-white wrist.

The child said something.

"What?" said the mother.

"Listen," the aunt said. "What did I tell you? What did I just now say?"

The Lady on the Cake

"SHE'S CALLED THE bride," the aunt said, holding the bride for the child to see (but not, of course, touch) in an effort at distraction.

The child, she thought, looked rather piqued.

"Bide?" he said.

"*Bride,*" she said. "The lady at the wedding on the icing on the cake. She was Mother's, of course. Mine, that is, my mother, and then, by extension, of course, your mother Elise's mother, too. Look," the aunt said. "Lovely."

"Up?" said the child.

"No," said the aunt. She raised the bride farther.

"Doll?" he said.

"No, no," the aunt said. "Mustn't touch." She put the bride up on the shelf, in place. Something was broken. She fingered the body.

"Auntie," the child said. "Bide?"

The aunt's hand shook. This was happening all too often to her. "As God is my witness," the aunt said. "Listen. What did your mother go and do?"

A Bedtime Tale

SHE WAS UNDER it all: knees raised and knobbed, the sheets a tent—stakeless, laundered—a house she had not built.

"Not," Elise said, "mine"—this voice of hers a hum, little more, a seepage of breath; it sounded to her as if located nowhere, spleenless. Here is where it was: beneath a hand. There was hair on her face. A fan up somewhere shaved the air, its blades old tin. All curve she was. She always had been—fetal, tight, and later rather ladylike and somewhat amiss. "Straighten yourself!" her mother had said. "Chin up!" Words, ink. Things had been balanced on top of her head. Britannica. Step by step, place to place, a headache of knowledge, of what she did not know. What a nomad she was, well thumbed—this house not hers, this fan refreshing nothing, useless, circling itself. She heard a flap of a sheet. A voice she heard, not hers said, "You," said, "you?"

She rolled, stilled, cheek against fabric. "Yes," she said in answer, and, answering again, said, "Do I what?"

Her hair was wet. She sat half sunk and puckering. She heard the knock. A piece of soap, papery, a peeling, a little bit of nothing, really, floated. There was something quite abrasive in her hand. She was loosening skin. Sloughing was what it was properly called. Gray in the tub, this stuff of her, rubbed off. Her legs were pink. Or nearly. Or rather, what they were was not so white. She lowered herself. The door—"Come out!"—was being worked. "Elise!" he said. "Come out, I said." How not to hear it? She opened her mouth. The taste was metallic. Down at the bottom, she felt the ring of dirt.

"A sliver, please," she said—made up and pinned, the hair in an attempt at an elaborate curl. "Less, please. Half of that," she said. Her fork was to the crystal. A toast was under way—lucky twosome!—the chandelier aglow. It was all of it heirloom, all hand-cut. "Only a drop," she said, "for me."

Applause in the ballroom.

The bride, aswoon, was drunk.

She was not the bride.

"Must you?" he said.

She was sniffing the flowers. She had been schooled. Discretion was the better part. She'd learned their names, promptly forgotten. Arms crossed over a flattened chest: "It's close in here," she said. "Is it not? Do you think?"

The fountain in the cake had gone askew.

What *were* they, in fact? Severely exotic genus of flowers? Purpled herbs? Bent grass?

She was at a window, a threshold—intemperate, the pain—hungover, and under a throw.

"Why can't you just stay put?" he said. "No faith," he said.

"Dear God," she said. A click of the jaw; she ground her teeth, averted, out of habit, her glance. This last trait was handed down; Mother had said it was not nice to look. Locked in one night, she had accidentally bloodied a casement, scarring a girlish fist. "Under my roof . . . ," her father had said, but that was someplace far from here. Of course, it was. The key ring, tickets: chronic, this misplacing jag. She did not look. A gypsy might have read into her past, all skin and fold. Her fortune: Travel; tall, dark gent.

"Tell me, am I right?" he said.

"You're right," she said. "I think." Although what was the question? Faithless in what? She was smoothing a wrinkle. Easy this, synthetic that, perfect for upkeep, preening under a wheeling blade. Still, it was humid, wasn't it?

He was chin into hands.

There was some kind of rule, some test. Was it fibers per inch? Knots per hour?

Surely Mother had told her this.

"Lovely," she'd said, regarding whatever, rounds of bread, the rice to toss; pumps to the floorboards, crossing her legs. A napkin with which she had tidied herself. The kiss was in her palm. Blotted. There were no two prints alike. She had been born this way, like this for this, singing, or rather mouthing, like a scout: Heigh-ho, nobody home, meat nor drink nor money have I none, still I will be . . . what? Sloughed to perfection? Holding her body like a glass full of wine? She could not eat that cake! "Very lovely," she'd said, a shade below whispering, running out again.

Oh, groom! Oh, florid relation!

She herself, not swift with words, had trusted in posture, relying on the value of a face. Intuiter, she sized the house. She minded his appearances. Sidelong, she saw him there in the bedroom, stubbled, in pain.

"Headache?" she said. "Eyeache? Toothache? Bloody itch?"

They were hospital corners, more or less.

"Some wedding," he said.

★   ★   ★

"Help me," she said. Let it be said that she was a woman who used herself, the skills she had been taught—nose to the cream pot, pinkie aloft, as if judging or maybe summoning rottage, touching a disinfected cut.

He had given her perfume, bath salts, mints.

When he was gone, she would stand on chairs—mother of necessity. The ladder backs as if in a salute to grand ancestral dead, not hers, and no, not his, retrieved from some false past. The rugs were Oriental.

"Help me, please," she said again, inventing, as ever, a need.

She stood at the sink.

She doused herself.

When he was gone, she would topple a bureau. Wall-to-wall, knots per bloody, knotty foot; inscrutable frictions, always, it seemed. She was always dragging something: her life in her head, clawed feet along the floor, a little track on the varnish—impossible to get to where she would.

She was that short.

"Perhaps it starts with *s,*" she said, still in the bathroom. "Statice or something. A lavender bud that my mother revered."

"Iris?" he said.

"Not iris," she said.

He sat on the tub lip.

He had often told her this: How often had he told her this: How was he to know? The things she asked! Was it taupe? Puce? Straw? Was it natural, this? Was it poly-whatever?

What was it that she smelled?

Whatever had she said?

What was she thinking?

"Fetch me a wafer, please," she said.

Was he to read her mind? Receded, as if in an emotional crease. Days, weeks. The hair in the face. No pride. Or was it shameless?

He gave her what she asked for.

She opened her mouth. She was back in the bed, why not? It was the place she had begun, in the hour of abandon—a rosy, absorbent, unholdable creature. Pulp, bone, labor, she had made this tent, inhabited it, again, again, tent upon tent, as if devoted to assembly: ghost town.

It was the body redressed.

He was questioning her.

There was all of her knowing at the tip of her tongue. Her breath, let out, dispersed.

She had listened to the whirring.

She was her witness.

It was she who, after all, had answered yes.

Squeal

"ONCE UPON A time," the aunt told the child, "there were three little pigs. And the first little pig—"

"Pig?" said the child.

"Yes, pig," said the aunt. "And the first little pig—"

"Oink," said the child.

"What?" said the aunt.

"Oink," said the child.

"Very well," said the aunt. "Fair enough," said the aunt. "Now, where is my glass?" She touched the wooden nightstand. It wobbled. "I need it," the aunt said. "Hear it? My larynx."

"Oink," said the child.

"Where?" said the aunt. "My glass," she said. "Things disappear. I swear it." She was searching the nightstand's surface with her hand. "Aha," she said. "Now, here we

34

are." She took a little swallow. "Where were we?" she said.

"We?" said the child. "Pig?"

"Why, of course," said the aunt. "Yes, pigs. And, as I was saying"—she stopped and took a sip, another sip—"and as I was saying, the three little not-so-thoughtful pigs—there came a day," the aunt said, "those little pigs, who'd been living rather well with their mother, high on the hog, if you will, with their mother, beautifully dressed, perfectly safe, what did they do? One fateful day? They left," the aunt said. "They up and left."

The aunt felt the child watching her. "Ran out," the aunt said. "Took off to seek their fortune, as pigs are apt to do. Here," she said. "Sit closer. Are you listening up? The mother of the pigs, of the first little pig and of the second little pig, and so forth, the heretofore indispensable mother was suffering distress, for they had broken her heart."

"Her hard?" said the child.

"Heart," said the aunt. "Do you know what that is? Your heart is what beats, your heart is the engine deep in your chest. Here," she said. "Inside." She touched the child's skin, on the child's rashy breast. The skin had been broken.

The child flinched.

"It hurts?" said the aunt. "Does it hurt, like this?"

The child said, "Mama."

"Mama," the aunt said. "As I was saying, the mother, of course—a sow, yes, a sow. Sow is the proper term, I think.

35

So let us say—here?" She tried again, the aunt did, to touch the child, who once again, in spite of her gentlest attentions, flinched.

"Listen," the aunt said. "Here? It hurts? Are you sweating?" she said. "Perspired? Tell me," the aunt said. "Look at you. What's wrong?"

The child said, "Mama."

The aunt said, "Where?"

"Where Mama is?" the child said.

"I told you," the aunt said. "Didn't I tell you? This is the story." The aunt took the tiniest bit of a swig. "As I was saying, as I am sure I have said before, the little pigs—one, two, three of them—abandoned their birthplace, leaving their mother to fend for herself, eager as eager pigs could be to run and seek their fortune. Do you hear?" the aunt said. "So the first little pig, such a smug little pig with a turned-up nose, was the first little pig to encounter—what? A man," the aunt said.

"Man?" the child said.

"A kind of peddler," the aunt said. "Traveling salesman. And what was he selling? Straw!"

"Sssss . . . ?" the child said.

"Straw," the aunt said. "Can you fancy it? Straw. Old, dry, bent straw. This man had naught to offer to the world save straw. 'Please, sir,' the pig squealed. 'Please, will you give me a bushel of straw with which to build a house?' For the first little pig had nary a sou," the aunt said.

"What sou is?" the child said.

"Listen," the aunt said. "What do you think? The first little pig was a thoroughly charming, engaging pig."

"Oink," said the child.

"As you've said," said the aunt. "Lazy. Ungrateful." She lifted her glass (her lips so dry!). "If pigs had wings," she said.

"Auntie?" the child said. "Auntie, some?" He touched the aunt's glass.

The aunt withdrew it quickly.

"Please," said the child.

"No," said the aunt.

"Drink?" said the child. "Some?"

"Not for you," the aunt said.

"Want it," the child said.

"This isn't what you think it is."

"Juice?"

"No juice," said the aunt. "This is gin."

"Gin?"

"As I said," said the aunt. "Now listen up. The first little pig—no, straw. The first little pig acquired, by questionable means, straw, and with this straw, the little pig assembled a house. Was this a good house? Was this house good?"

"Mama?" the child said.

"No," said the aunt. "Not good. For the big, bad wolf was lurking about. The big, bad wolf—"

"Woof," said the child.

"Wolf," said the aunt. "Big, bad."

"Bad," said the child.

"Wolf," said the aunt.

The child, "What wolf is?"

The aunt looked straight at the child's face, in the child's eyes. "Didn't she teach you anything? Evil," she said. "Do you think this is funny? This is not funny. Listen up. The big, bad wolf approached the house, the house of straw, came up to the window, up to no good, and here is what he said. He said, 'Out, come out, come out, little pig! I know you're there.' But the first little pig, a wily pig, well-schooled, in fact, knew this: The wolf had teeth. The wolf had eyes. The wolf was possessed of a heat in the belly. 'No,' said the pig, the first little pig, in a high-pitched voice. 'I won't come out nor show my face. Not by the hair of my chinny chin chin!'"

The child, it somehow seemed to the aunt, was suppressing a facial expression the aunt did not like.

"Listen," the aunt said. "This is not funny. Not one bit. Not with evil lurking about. This is what the wolf said: 'I'll huff and I'll puff and I'll blow—'"

"Where Mama is?" the child said.

"I told you," the aunt said. "Don't try my patience. The big, bad wolf was entirely angry. The big, bad—"

"Mama," the child said.

The aunt drew in a considerable breath, wasted, she presumed, on the child.

"I want her," the child said.

The aunt said, "I know it."

"Mama," the child said.

"Sleeping," the aunt said. "Sleeping, as ever. Elsewhere, as ever. Why doesn't anyone listen to me?"

The child's face reddened.

She touched the damp brow. She held the sweating glass to it.

He opened his mouth.

"I'll huff," she said.

"Huff," he said.

"Puff," she said. "Here." She angled the glass for the child to take a sip. "Puff," she said.

"Co——," he said.

"What?" she said. "Swallow."

The child seemed to shudder.

"Right," said the aunt. "And that was that. The last that was heard of the first little pig. The pig was dead. But this, of course, is nothing approaching the end of the story. The next little pig, the second little pig"—she turned to the child—"What? Is it cold? The second little pig encountered a man whose trade in life was sticks. Sticks! 'Please, sir,' the pig squealed, 'may I have a bundle of sticks, please, for sticking together a house?' Well, the second little pig was a tricky little pig, an insouciant pig, and so the sticks were given. Presented. And what do you think? Was this house good? A moment, please," the aunt said. She drank.

"Please," said the child. "More?"

"Well," said the aunt. "Just a sip, then. One more sip. Don't slurp." She blotted the liquid from underneath the mouth. "Now, the big, bad wolf, still up to no good, no good at all," the aunt said, "showed up at the house of the second little pig. This house, you'll recall, consisted of straw."

"Sticks," said the child.

"Whichever," the aunt said. "'Out! Come out!' the pig— I mean, the wolf—yelled. And what do you suppose?"

"No," said the child.

"No?" said the aunt. "No is no answer. The answer," the aunt said: "The pig would not budge. Not one inch. One bloody iota. And so," the aunt said, "the big, bad wolf huffed and he puffed and—"

"Stop it," the child said.

"—blew," said the aunt. "He blew the house in."

"No, no," said the child.

"Yes, yes," said the aunt.

"Where pig went?" the child said.

"Dead."

The child was looking rather decidedly worse to the aunt. "Where Mama is?" the child said.

"Don't be thankless," the aunt said. "Didn't I tell you? Listen," she said. "Listen. Now listen. Just listen to me. Really, I ask, can a person tell a story?" She raised the glass. She tipped it back. "Now, the third little pig, the final," the aunt said, "last, and allegedly wise little pig constructed a house of stone."

40

"Sssss," said the child.

"What sss," said the aunt. "Stone, rock—whichever. I can't recollect to be honest. Closer, please," the aunt said. She grasped the child's hand, the too-thin wrist. "Sit still and let me finish. Who should appear at the pig's stone house, still evil, unsated, not ever to be satisfied—'Out! Come out, come out—'"

"No," said the child.

"And the third little pig said—"

"Hide," said the child.

"Huff," said the aunt.

"Run," said the child.

"So the third little pig squealed, 'Not by the hair of my chinny chin chin!' Still think this is funny?" the aunt said. "'Not by the hair of my chinny chin chin.'" The child shook his head. "So," said the aunt. "The big, bad wolf said, 'I'll huff and I'll puff and I'll blow you apart.' Huff, huff, huff," said the aunt. "But the big, bad wolf huffed and he puffed and the house stood fast. The house would not crumble. The wolf would not quit. The wolf vowed then to come in through the chimney."

"Chinny?" the child said.

"Chimney," the aunt said. "The place where the smoke escapes. But the third little pig, the third, purportedly wise little pig, laid a great big pot of boiling water under the chimney, down in the coal bed, deep in the coal."

"Co——," said the child.

"Gracious, you're trembling," the aunt said. "Have another sip. A final, little medicinal sip." The child winced. "Ah," she said. "The big, bad wolf flew in through the chimney, down through the chimney, and fell through the chimney, and into the pot. Kaboom," said the aunt. "Burned to death. Dead in the pot. The beast in the ashes," the aunt said. "No? Some fortune," the aunt said. "Listen to me. That pig should have never left home in the first place."

"Auntie?" the child said.

"What?" said the aunt. "What's cold?" said the aunt. "For heaven's sake, speak up."

A Note About Volume

"AT LAST," THE aunt said. "Why, at last," the aunt said. "I like a moment to myself, you know. Listen, what with all the commotion, the comings and goings day and night in this house. Impossible. First of all, Father, and now her— Elise—I can hear her in the hall again, looking for something, searching, I think, or else carrying something, or tending to something, or pacing. She is pacing in the hall again, isn't she, now? Someone is coughing. The walls of this house are too entirely thin. I hear through wood. Easy. The water is gentle. I take a bit of scent in it, as Mother once did. A person must refresh herself, what with the heat. Mother, you know, would wash us and scrub us both to a pink, Elise and myself, together in here. Our knees were apt to touch in here. Elise was apt to flinch. Smaller than I, the delicate sister—thin now, the clothes gone slack and in rags about the body. If Mother could see her. As if by her leaving, as if the way Elise left, out through the window, she hadn't killed Mother enough by then. Rags she wears. And as for him, that child of hers—why, save us all! What is there to say to him, to try to tell Father? I try to distract him. I do what I can. A person is human, aren't I now? I like to take a soak, you know. A balm for the skin, and with something to drink. I get thirsty in here. The water encourages thirst, and what with the child taxing my throat to tell him a story. Look at my flesh. Just look at my flesh. These arms of mine! The places no one sees of me. Oh! The body will soften in water. Skin will fall away from me, and knuckles turn color from washing myself. Mother liked to wash in here. She never let us enter. Once, in fact, just once, in fact, Mother remained here the length of the day. It was Father, of course, in the evening who took her. She heard him, she said. She had heard him, she said. She liked to use a scented talc—lily or lilac or something like that—to powder her nose. The child needs to bathe, of course; the skin has erupted. Not just the weather and travel and light, as she, Elise, insists upon, as if she even looks at him. The child is coughing blood, you know. Mother was distressed with her. Of course she was. The way she let things spill and burn. And Mother's poor nerves! How Mother tried always, again, to amend her. Father spoke of someplace else when speaking to Mother. Nights he cries, the child does. And what am I to do for it, save bathe again, save pace again when I cannot sleep? I cannot sleep. Her breath is in the water here, a stain on the tile. The train goes by too loudly in the night, the whistle as if it were summoning us. Elise went and answered. Father is breathing loudly in the dark. He used to call out to her, to Mother, in sleep, and I would hear him in the hall. There is something in the woodwork, the pantry, I think. The water is warm. I finger-test, as Mother did, for safety and such. A floral scent is what I like. She and I, Elise and I, both used to bathe here, together in here, until we were clean, for the moment, at least. The child is unsanitary, not that I say so. I am no mother, as she has said. The child cries. The cloth is nice and fresh and white. Lovely," she said.

The aunt turned the spigot off. She entered the tub. Her body made the water overflow.

Must I Tell You Again?

SHE HEARD THE boy's voice. Of this, Elise was certain. She heard it—his voice, him, the boy—up again, awake again, if scarcely. This she knew. This room—hers—once hers, unassembled by night—still night, too damp, her nightdress damp—appeared mostly lightless. "Yes," she said, awakening to what? The boy's high voice sounded injured to her, as if pitched from a dream.

The sheet began to fall.

The glass, at least, was cool. She lifted it. She drank—a tonic, fizzless—spilled it, a toast to the house. "Yes?" she said. She felt for him, this boy of hers. Tip of the finger, tip of the tongue—spitting, the image. The room re-formed.

"Mama?" he said.

"What is it?" she said.

Floor, lamp, bureau.

What was the question? And why did she always say yes, of course? Rags, a shoe, shirt off the back: an opened drawer. In view of the fever, the fact, the likely fact of the fever, which, it seemed, the boy still ran—and she herself, why, she herself, she felt herself, wetted and heated—a bit lip besotted, unsuckleable—and always, still, the whistle at the window ("Go?" he said, has said, "go?" this boy she had carried, soaking, carried away and wrenched), in view of the fever, rashy chest, ungenerous infection—yes, she said. What else?

Why, of course.

The aunt told stories nightly.

She—the boy's mother—was certain, or as certain as a person could be, that this was true.

"Co——," the boy said, "co" or "coal" or "cold."

"Cold?" she said.

"No," he said.

"Lie quiet," she said. Cheek. Chin. Blown breath. A bundle of fabric. "Dreams," she said. "You were dreaming, you know. Were you dreaming again? Tell me. You must tell me. Tell me what."

What story is this?

Insurgent mercy: "No," he said, unfolding.

"You must tell me," she said.

("Must you?" she had said. "Must you tell me?" she'd said, some bygone time. She'd seen her lover's teeth, inhaled the sulfurous breath. "Why leave a person twice?" he'd said.

"Why bother to stay when I'll leave you again? There," he'd said. "Here," she'd said. "Once," she'd said. "Once upon a time," she'd said—or some such. "James? Yes?" The answering bidden and brokered in the query, father but a twinkle in the eye of the child, going, going, gone.)

"No," the boy said.

"James," she said.

"Jim," she said.

"No," he said.

"Huff," he said.

"Baby?" she said. "I know this story, too," she said. "I think."

"Huff, huff, huff," he said.

"I'll huff and I'll puff?" she said.

"Listen," she said. The air in the room smelled dankly of him—or of her, perhaps, some part of her: curled hair, not washed, the too-traveled nightdress, bliss sopped up.

"Listen, Auntie drinks," she said. "She mustn't be trusted. You oughtn't to trust her. I never did trust her. There," she said. "Rest," she said. "Poor dear Mother. Rest her soul."

"Now I lay me down," she had said, a prayer, a come-on.

The bed unmade itself. It was all of it taken. He, the boy, had turned from her. And there she lay, laid bare by him—James, Jim, Baby, boy, boy, boy she had borne, as in absence invoked, in a stutter of the body, breeched release, the belly unwilling, or willing death. The cord about the throat. Oh, embrace me. "James?" she'd said. "Mother?" A willful undoing. Hands. A cry. The rattle of a window. "Mother," she'd said, receiving herself. A knot was tied. And at the breast, a liquid not quite milk began to leak.

The boy's eyes were closed.

"Sweet," she said. She covered herself, inadequately. She'd named the boy and touched the boy and held the boy as if he were a body she could hold.

She was clutching a sheet.

"If," she had said. "If, if, if." she'd said. "If I die before I wake," but she'd been a girl then, cheek to the curtain, stoking the urge.

("Just dreams, you had. Sweet thing," he'd said, her nightly guide, made seeable only in motion, it seemed—the lover turned father lit out.)

The boy seemed to shudder.

"Rest," she said.

"Sweet thing," she said, the lover's voice revealed in her. She loved the boy's fear, or rather, the moment of feeling she could somehow contain it, consume it.

"There," she said.

The glass had been emptied.

The child's mouth opened. He opened his eyes.

"Listen," she said. "Do you hear me?" she said. She brought herself in view of him, by way of an instinct. Bloody itch. "There's no such thing, whatever it is. Rest," she said. "Be still," she said. "The day's about to break."

Part Two

NIGHT AT LAST

Sweet

SHE WAS BORN in December in Baraboo or there-
abouts—small, still, blue, a girl, and, by some trick of oxy-
gen, alive.

She lived to marry late. She bore descendants—visions,
of sorts—herself transformed, and she herself, by way of
them, in view of them, transported irretrievably. Girls, of
course. Elise, yes, and yes, of course, the older, the sister—
dress and brush and kiss and tell. This is the story: Night at
last. The tucking in. "Once upon a time . . ." and was it pigs
or was it bears or something altogether else? It was all of it,
always, it seemed, about shelter.

Listen up. Look at her: at work in the pantry, impeccably
laced—robe, hair, rib—a baster of meat, of scrap.

"Mother," they call.

These are items she loves: a ring, the linens, curtains at
a window, lilac or some such flower as that.

There is a light she despises.

They want her to look. "Mother," they call her. "Sweet. Come here."

And here she is, as if sniffing the gauze, as if under the glass.

Someone is snuffling, always, it seems.

"Like so," she says, adjusting a finger, a thumb, one hand, two hands: "Here is the church and here is the steeple, open the doors—" and what? Keep what?

There's a whistle in the not-too-distant distance, a chill in the room.

"What is it?" she says. And where have they got to—one, two, three of them, husband and offspring?

"Tell me," she says.

Who is sleeping in the chair? Who is breathing on the pillow? What in the world has been spilling in the kitchen?

"Tell me," she says. And hasn't she said this more than once, twice, in some untidiable past? Roving again, she holds herself, arms full of bedding and other violently laundered belongings, stanching the flow, mopping a floor, a brow, a whetted body. "Girls!" she calls. "Girls?"

The voice is what fails her, and also the riotous pulse at the wrist, and also, of course, the present moment.

"Sweet," she said, sweetly.

Open the hand, and here were the people.

Here was the cake, the knife, the bride.

Here was the coldest sheet.

Abandon

NIGHT AT LAST, the aunt thought. The child, at least
for the moment, at rest, embraced by a dream or a stillness,
the aunt thought, or solely the empty repose of fatigue, and
she herself relieved of a self-imposed duty: teller of the
story, huffer and puffer, and ever-questioned guardian, wolf
in fair clothing—until the child awoke.

It was close in the house. A tissue the aunt had nestled—
discretely, she hoped—between her breasts (she felt it, the
way that her breasts surely fell—no infant nursed nor lifted
gaze, no milk with which to sate a throat, to plumpen or,
rather, to deepen a leg crease. yet gravity received her, wooed
her, the aunt thought, as if in rebuke) was softened, damp.
She fingered it. Of course, she did. No one was looking.
Pink, this tissue. Pink, of course. She knew without duly
seeing the thing, as if sensing its color from under her flesh,

as if somehow the object had issued from blood, some mineral inheritance, as if, perhaps, of Mother's iron taste—an inborn impulse—for Mother had chosen only soporific hues: purse, blush, pale dress, a tissue tucked into a willfully lovely and, most likely, woolly pocket. Seeping. Go on. Summon her. Talc, breath, the dream of an effluvium.

Enter.

This is Mother's room. Or rather, it had been.

Not much touched.

Thick of night, still of night, no way to make this night new. Night notwithstanding, it seemed to the aunt to be altogether closer than ever.

Quiet, the aunt thought, seemed to swell.

She dabbed about her rutting brow.

It felt to her as if light of the day had heated the wood, the moldings, tired appointments; as if, as well, it had saturated crevices, and darkened and blackened and fueled this house.

The aunt paced, wakeful. Room to room, here to here, no place to go to, nursing a friction under her feet (she walked in Mother's pinkish slippers, lifted out of Mother's room—not quite hers—a loan, of sorts, for the foreseeable duration: pricey and undeniably snug), arms to the rib cage, pulse in the head, a bead she did not blot.

Father slept. Of course, he did. She could have foretold this. In a sweat in the chair, in recline, yet active, as if, the aunt thought, he could almost simply be roused into discourse. Listen! Behold! The breath of the man, in the middle of the night, obstructed and in-blown. She, the aunt, of course, stopped. Attentive as ever, she stood at the foot of the chair with the intention to hear and overhear him, nodded, uttered: "Sawing wood, he is," she said, or some such overheard expression. (Ear to a doorknob, praying to shrink, she had been a thoughtful or, at least, a conscientious child. Not like some. Not, of course, to name a name. Look not to her to be rattling mothballs.) "Listen," she said, addressing herself. Father snored. Noisy, disruptive, loud, the aunt thought—but not enough to wake the dead.

Sweet.

A flutter arose that the aunt could not suppress.

"Excuse," she said to no response. Undoubtedly infectious—the air in the palm of the hand.

She had coughed.

She had, in fact, made, as Mother would have judged it, a rather entirely unladylike harrumph. This, the aunt thought, is the sound of a woman awake in a house full of sleep, this plea or this apology rendered, submitted in the night as if to someone all-knowingly present and alert.

Ring, the aunt thought, in her appraisal of Father.

Lamp.

A bulb.

A slipper.

Buds. (But were they iris? Or lilies? Or were they rightly lilac?)

A sweetly lovely morsel.

Goblets to sip from (crystal—listen: the elegant timbre!).

Rice.

Lace.

A claw-foot tub.

Unbudgeable bureau.

Towels (imported).

Window sash.

Rebuffed parquet, and so forth.

Trappings (inviolate, fine)—the aunt had furnished Father's dreams again, retrieved and replaced things, conceiving a vision the eye might fix.

These, of course, were not enough.

There were, to be certain, sheets.

A gauzy curtain, unflappable by wind or any plausible—or otherwise—intrusion.

The silver, aglimmer and wrought.

Such patent wealth! Such impeccable, the aunt thought, accoutrements as might have been hoarded by Mother—and yet there was unignorably this: The walls plain shook. Soot entered and settled. The house was in a most, as Mother had deemed it, ungenial location, too near to the tracks. "Such a shame," she had said. "Is it not?" she had said, insistent, recrossing and tucking her legs.

The aunt, of late, could not but walk. She walked. Her arches had fallen, her toes—pinched, damp—were ineffectively powdered. Chafing, she walked, regarded the sleepers: James, Jim, Baby, the child, turned to his mother—her sister,

Elise—so undistressed, her arm flung, loose. Sleep was what the aunt smelled; she made to inhale it. ("I'll huff and I'll puff," she had said to the child, and what had he, in turn, done? Why, questioned her! "What is a wolf? A chimney? What is straw?" It was as if, the aunt thought, he had come up out of nowhere, carrying nothing—save, of course, the toy, which was unquestionably missing—ragged, with a fever, not a shirt on the back, unspoken for, apparently, and yet, the aunt was made to concede it, possessed, in the brow, in the lip, in the rigid little mien, of certain indelible family traits.)

Elise, it appeared to the aunt, had been sleeping like a baby—out like a light, a bump on a log, and so on—fancy that! Why, look at them! Sister, nephew ("What is coal?" the child had said, or rather, "What coal is?" This speech of his, the aunt thought, as if in translation, no?) languid, and ever so faintly discerned: a tinge, a breath, just slightly dank, their contours seeable vaguely, by way of a window, lit from without.

Heat, the aunt thought, had adhered to the night, expansive, diffuse, and at odds with a rational person's ability (such as herself, for example) to think.

Reckless, the aunt thought, the way heat bloomed—grew? rose?—as if out of the wood, and also, as well, from the child's flesh (undoubtedly red, abraded, sight unseen notwithstanding); and also, it rankled below a leveled breast—salt to a tissue, a robe too tight. Said garment, of course, had been the property of Mother. Carriage mattered, made or broke a fit. (Weight to the flattest part of the skull was how the aunt had learned to step: curl, leaf, bound spine—"Up," said Mother, "chin up, up"—scarcely a child, the aunt had been, straightened, instructed, groomed, she had wrongly believed, encyclopedically.) Mother strode in rosy tones, prim-lipped, appropriate, a bosom supported, comported unobtrusively, a rhyme before bedtime ("Here is the church and here is the steeple . . ."), always, in hand, the sanctioned treat: dainty and risen and floridly iced. "Here," said Mother. "Here, have some, have less."

There was always a napkin or doily. Additionally:

A peck on a cheek.

A doll on a shelf.

A pinkened spot—apparently lipstick.

She, the aunt, could guess her weight, her tutored, dependable, not-faint tread. There was something quicker afoot than she.

"Again?" she said. Some being at work in the twill of a fabric, rot in the molding—industrious, unpoisoned, the aunt thought, impervious to heat, or even energized, and frenzied, in need. She, the aunt, continued on, unsettled.

Here again: reduced, revealed, and quick on the uptake. "Papa," she says, replacing herself. So young she is! Backtracked. To sit—oh bliss!—in a lap; she hears through the wall of rib—a heart. Father. A resting place, but not for long; strong arms shall raise her. Look: She rides him piggyback; Father's shoulder is muscled still; she moves at an angle, laughing (the aunt, not yet, of course, the aunt, indisputably laughing), chin to a cowlick, ankle engaged, the hand in no way yet infirm, a heat from the breath from within.

A squeal.

There comes, as if unanswering a prayer, a smaller and daintier version of her, unjoyously witnessed. ("Here," said Mother. "Here is the church and here is the steeple, open the doors. I said, 'open the doors.' . . .")

Nothing suffices—fluid in the mouth, nor tongue; lips thinned and dry; a dry hand, dank wall, this house—so ill kept up!

The cough again, unhelpable.

The aunt was quite flushed.

There was something desired—some warm thing, she told herself, a drop, a nip (a word she had gleaned while gleaning, tucked—a child and then some, prone, blessed, infusable, inclined to absorb them, Father and Mother: smoke, air, perfume, a chemical disbursement, teeth to the newly minted tongue).

Milk, perhaps, could do the trick.

(Except, if the aunt recalled it correctly, the milk was all dried.)

Mother had served up coddled milk, or clotted cream, or steam, a bit of cake. "Sleep," she had offered, the moral of the story, an end. Such children, both in the pink, in the white of the bed, Elise, of course, smaller, and she, on that count, smaller too—a chin not yet doubled, a middle unthickened; Mother, of course, alive still, hand to a fore-head, palliative. "Mustn't," said Mother, "snuffle on silk."

She the aunt, had heeded—inch upon inch, foot upon foot—respectful, detached and, in the night, removed.

This was not her shabby cloth.

Sticks and such could break her bones, but this was not the aunt's flesh, the aunt's blood, soiling the bedding.

Not her bed.

Nor would she lie here.

Bearing, the aunt thought, posture and habit—these were hers—a cough, a hiccough (or rather, perhaps, to be thoroughly frank, a slight burp), a rare thirst, unquenchable.

For she had labored—ceaseless.

He, the child, James, Jim, Baby—imagine!—had offered correction: The house had no chimney, the child had said, nor even furthermore a brick. ("Why three of them?" the child had said, as if he could tally.)

The breast lay unsuckled.

The child lay stirring.

Elise plain slept.

And Father: By Father, the aunt stood tall—in thought, of course, as was her wont. Stone, she thought. Why, yes, she thought, assessing him, stone, in fact, glimmered, refractive, at least in the wake of a blown kiss, a last wave—a jeweled hand, bedazzling . . . receding.

Unshaken, the aunt thought.

In this she would not lie.

Q&A

Q. Was there really a gemstone hidden on the premises?
A. Yes.

I'll Huff and I'll Puff

THE ROOM WAS dark. Not known to him. Bestirred, if not yet fully alert, he rubbed his eyes (the fevered lids), pressed them. Face to the linen (exquisitely threaded, unbeknown, of course, to him, unlaundered, discolored), he registered a smell.

The air held disturbance.

Someone had entered, it seemed to him.

"Mama?" he said.

"Mama?" he said, aflinch at a nostril.

"Mama!"

"Papa?" the aunt said. "What are you doing?"

★   ★   ★

The train carried oil, lumber, and coal. The doors slid open. The coal was not covered. Night was devoted to freight, of course, and, by necessity, to men.

"Sweet," said Father, embracing himself.

To see him, the aunt thought, or rather to smell him—reeking in the night: asleep, perhaps, maybe sleeping in motion.

Ash fell.

Smoke rose.

"Stop it," the aunt said. "Didn't you hear me? What are you doing standing here?"

"Come," said the lover.

She'd come to the window—half dressed, ungrown. "Listen," Elise said. "Hear it now?"

"Of course I do," her sister said. "So?"

The lamp, in the shape of a lady, had a shade made of lace. The lamp had been lit.

The lace had been apparently affected by heat.

★   ★   ★

"Hush," said the mother.

"There," said the mother.

"Once upon a time," she said, or some such over-turned expression. "Once, in a house such as this, perhaps, lived three little oh-so-fancy pigs.

"Please," said the mother. "The three little pigs abided in comfort. The first little pig—

"What?" said the mother. "Fire?"

The sound the mother heard sounded only like rumbling, the transport of night.

"Burn," said the child. He tugged at the mother.

"Oh," said the mother. "Tell me the truth. Has somebody ruined the ending for you?"

"Yes?" said the mother.

"Go?" said the child. The room seemed to move to him.

"No matter," said the mother. "It happens every night."

"Papa," the aunt said. "Listen to me."

"Now I lay me down," she said. A girl still, Elise was—kneeling, reciting by rote. She made a tired motion.

"Cover your mouth," her sister said. "You know that's not polite."

The air seemed to him as if someone had opened a door to a room where a window was cracked.

The air held soot.

"Lily of the valley"—the mother of the aunt and of the mother of the child, et cetera, had offered this: a suitable flower for sacred occasions, weddings and such. Yes? Or was it another genus? Statice? Iris? Queen Anne's lace? And how, the aunt thought, was a person, a dutiful person such as herself, to recall this distinction, what with the din of professional solace?

The lace, it appeared, had been soiled as well.

"If," she said. "If I die before I wake . . . ," not yet a mother, untaken, aroused.

The lover slept as if unborn.
    "Shhh," she said.

"Do you hear me?" she said.

A fan above her whirred, revolved.

Her belly rose. A strange heart was beating and beating inside her.

Fighting for cover, she let out a breath.

"Please," she said.

"Papa, please," the aunt said. She saw the burned nails.

He turned to her, the aunt saw—arteried, gutted, the innards rising out of him, more mineral than sinew, a cigarette in hand.

"It's dangerous," the aunt said.

"Mama?" the child said. "Mama? Mama?"

The child began to cough and then to wheeze.

"Bless you," the aunt said, entering the room.

"The cigarette," the aunt said. She pressed a wetted rag to the child's face and, lightly, over his nose.

"Mama?" he said.

"Breathe," the aunt said. "Floral. Inhale it. Ah, lovely, isn't it?"

The child smelled fluid.

★   ★   ★

The aunt made a gesture.

"Knock on wood," she said.

Father retreated, smoldered at a fingertip.

The curtain had lifted. The window was open.

And so Elise had, almost imperceptibly, gone.

Steeple

"WAIT," SAID THE aunt. "Here is the church. No, wait," she said.

The child leaned into her. His breath smelled rather chemical or animal to her.

"Like so," she said, entwining her fingers.

"Auntie?" he said.

He covered his eyes.

She raised her palms. "How did Mother do this?" she said.

The Aunt Sweeps

"I SWEEP," THE aunt said. "Not that you'd know by the look of the place. Why, look at the place. Just look at the place! Rice, yeast, whatever it is, spilled all about, smeared about, stepped on—sugar or some such. How does it happen? Almost as if there were spillage in the night, someone entering the pantry, and clumsy to boot. I sweep, you know. You'd think I was the serving girl. Listen, you'd think for the labor involved, you'd think it was mine, this house, and me the rightful mistress. It's Father's house. Rest assured, this isn't my house. No sirree. I dust too. I try, at least. Supposing he'd notice—Father, that is, asleep or whatever he is in the chair. Not saying much. Or speaking to someone— who knows who? 'Sweet,' he says or 'cigarettes' or 'rags,' or even he says, 'Auntie'—'Auntie,' he calls out, 'come to me and bring me this and fetch me that.' He takes a drink too, you know. He always did, a drop or two. Even when Mother—when Mother was alive. If Mother could see this—Father like this, reclined again, and him, the child, the boy, of course, James, Jim, Baby, whatever you will, whichever he goes by. She, of course, is gone again, likely out the window. Elise. My head hurts to think of her. The night Elise left—the first time Elise left, slipped out the window, I saw it—I held my tongue, I must admit, I kept my own counsel. This is the truth—well before the boy was born; at least, now, I think so, to judge by the size of him— oh, such a leaving. The house was wild with grief. Frantic. Mother, God rest her, ruined a lamp. She tore and she broke things. Beautiful things such as Mother had treasured: chips, scraps—she mended them, of course, in time, but never completely. Seams in the china, and so forth— cracks, the little signs of forced repair. And anyway, all of it only replacements for everything Father had long ago lost. No word from her, not one. I mean, Elise, of course— selfish of her—but no, I won't say it. Seal your lips, as Mother said. Never kiss and tell was another of her sayings. Who would I tell? Father said, 'Don't speak of this.' Well, surely, we spoke of it. How in the world is a person not to speak? Father held forth. He spoke quite often, in fact, of the missing and the dead. It was a habit of his. Mother was terribly fragile by then, and she was always very sensitive. She slept in Elise's room, at least on occasion, upsetting herself. The train seemed to rankle her, and also the air and the weather and dust. Smells, too, rattled her. I dust this house. I've mentioned this, haven't I? Mother was immaculate. Hospital corners. Polish—not optional. White gloves, soap. Why, soap, of course. A house must be scrubbed now and then—in fact, often. Impossible to stop it—soot from the window, the train, motes. And how can a person, such as myself, for example, keep up with it all, along with looking after Father, and him—the child—poor sickly thing, and me not in excellent health myself? I cough, you know. My larynx. It takes my peace of mind away. Yes? I cover my mouth. I urge the child to do likewise. Not that it helps. His brow is surely ours, of us, but as for the rest of him—clearly the spitting image of somebody else. Some wet-mouthed lover, I'll warrant, a vision of Elise's in the thrall of the night—her wayward groom. My, what a vision. Tall, dark, a traveler. I might as well imagine it, mightn't I, now? The child is quite a sight, you know—first of all, the rash, which she, of course, neglected. Elise—the fever, the bloody cough and skin. And now he is sallow, sallow as well. The shame of it. Pity, in the second place. The pity of it. I tend to him, I do, you know. I wash the boy—sometimes. I feed the boy as best I can. Not but bones and skin, he is. Not like us. We had to flush out the bones. Children, I tell you. Elise and myself. We liked to look in Mother's room. We lifted the lampshade—Mother's lovely frilly one, to get to the bulb. We brought our hands up to it—the heat and the light of the bulb, all the better to witness the bones through skin.

Our hands were red, held up like this. The bones were plainly visible, alive in the light, then hidden again. Our bodies concealed us. Now the veins have risen like bones in my hands. My hands look like Father's. The lamp now is broken. I've mentioned the fact. Mother, I think, if truth be told, detested it. She never did tell me. The shade, as I have said, was made of lace, fine lace, and the top was made of porcelain, a delicate cheek, a rosy breast—it was a lamp, as you know, in the shape of a lady, the shade her skirt. The light was rather weak, and for the fact of the matter, such a lamp as this is not made anyplace in the world anymore, as far as I know. Not as if I leave this house, save to meet the train on occasion. I rarely set foot. Mother would light it at bedtime for us. It was heaven, almost, to lie on her pillow, and Mother would move us in our sleep. She would tell us a story—creatures of the wood or else maybe a maiden, a spindle. The kiss. There was always a house, and often blood. She'd tuck us in, Mother. She'd come to us mornings. She fed us crustless bread and such. Biscuits. Tea. She taught us comportment—to stand and to sit, and also to rise in the appropriate manner from a chair. She taught us how to cross our legs. Jellies, she fed us. Elise paid no nevermind. Forever at the window. Always at the window. Pressed to the window, waiting for it—the whistle in the night. She learned to lie down. 'Oh,' she said, 'listen.' 'Oh,' she said. 'Feel.' I still feel the breath of her, Mother's minty breath in her. 'Hear it?' she said. I heard the train's passing.

Someone was beckoning her in the night. I understood. I've thought of someone too, you know, a man, I will warrant. I am not simple. Mother never knew, of course. She straightened my collar. 'Chin up,' she'd tell me, a book on my head. 'Develop the muscle. There you go.' Father was tall in his gait back then. Not at all the way you see him sitting here now. He could open a room with the sound of his voice. 'Listen,' he'd say. He liked to tell stories of where he had been, the country he'd come from, ashes now, of course, he'd say—burnt roads, shoes lost, a house passed by gone up in flames. A city of the dead. Someone, a woman, he told us, had died of the exertion of trying to pull a child from the rubble. The child died too, of course. A dog died of heartbreak, abandoned on a road. Father said the feet were bloody, ragged, he said. His siblings were missing, an aunt who had been like a mother to him. 'Gone,' he would say to whoever was sitting on his lap—Elise, of course, and I, too. 'Paper valises,' Father would say. 'Only what was on our backs. A river of fire.' Nothing to mark the occasion, the ones who had vanished. A person, he told me, was buried alive—at night, I would see her, alive in the earth, the weight of the earth like a lover on her. I never, ever spoke of it, never with Father. It might have been a man, of course. Mother said always, 'Save your breath. What are you thinking, what are you doing, telling a child a story like this, such a story as this?' And Mother would hush him and hush us and bring us a drink. and him a drink, a cool drink, a damp cloth, and speak of something else again, a flower in a garden. Mother could soothe him—almost, I think. She'd mop his brow. Wash things. I wash, you know. I wash this house. Not that you'd know it. The house collects dirt, what with the child and also what with the mice, of course, and what with whatever it is that is living in the pantry. Things are bitten, torn apart. The floor, I believe, has been permanently damaged. Walls, too—the walls are streaked, as if someone has been feeling the way in the middle of the night, as if in need of support or unable to see. And also, as well, as if I don't have enough to contend with, the child appears to be waking in the night. Or he is talking in sleep. I am afraid to find out. 'Coal,' he says, 'coal,' as if he is remembering or maybe reliving. Or maybe he is saying something else. 'Go'? Is he yearning to wander away from here? He is muffled in sleep, or not asleep, whichever it is. He is getting out of bed. He is searching for something—not, it seems, Elise, but what I can't tell you. Hungry and thirsty all day long. All bones, he is. I own to a certain thirst myself. It's heat, you know. Heat and labor. And what do I do with the child in the night, save wipe his brow, save tell him a story? Always this, as best I can. 'Auntie,' he says. 'Auntie, auntie. Say it,' he says. The child, of course, repeats himself. It has to do with age, I guess. He doesn't know how old he is, or else he won't tell me. Blood in the cough. There is blood in the cough, and what am I to do for it? Elise has simply gone again. I might have foretold this. Of course, she went. Why wouldn't she? A person never changes much—save, of course, Father. Save Father after Mother. Always in motion, clever little sister, thief. But what has she taken? Nothing of value as far as I know. I have looked, I have looked. Emptied the drawers. Closets. Shelves. The linens are accounted for. Purses. Clothes— well, after all, they were all of them heavy, Mother's garments, for Mother never summered, never in her life. Hats were wrapped as new in there. Reeking of mothballs. Skins, she liked, and silk, of course, and worsteds, rather unusually dyed. And Father? What of his effects? A shirt, perhaps, the pocket change. The papers are useless: name, age, a false year. Father's shoes are stained again, unwearable. I polish what I can. I tend to the woodwork as Mother once showed me. Buff things up. Mother came from someplace else. She told me this: There in the winter, you breathe and see your breath; the breath turns to steam, she said, or ice again— and snow, she said. Impenetrable drifts of it. This house was built to last. Mother would say this, dusting a molding, or maybe a sill or a ledge. Chamois, she swore by, even in the powder room. She taught me to freshen. What with the train and now with what surely are vermin, and all the debris, the ash from Father's cigarettes—the filth of it. Nothing is in order here. A fixture is broken. A drawer is stuck. The hinges are calamitous. Father misses all of it, or makes believe. It used to be Father would start at almost anything: a whistle, a step in the dark of the hall. 'Listen,' he'd say. 'Just listen to me. Allow me to tell you a thing or two, a tale, a joke. Knock, knock.' Father could laugh, you know. I never guessed rightly. 'Yoo-hoo,' he'd say. 'One,' he'd say. 'Two. I am counting,' he'd say. I hid behind the furnishings or maybe in a closet or under a bed. Father would find me. 'You,' he'd say. 'Come sit with me. Let me tell you a story of someplace else.' Skies dark from smokestacks, a factory, a ruin of clay. Mother kept a tally of provisions in the house. As in an inventory. China and silver, a towel, slippers, a morsel in the pantry. Buds—nipped. Pruned in time. For Mother loved flowers, as I have mentioned, adored an arrangement. Lilies, I think, or something. I never had the head for it. Violet? Lilac? Some sort of perishable bud as that. She held her nose so close to them, deep in the center. She sneezed, too, coughed a bit. Her eyes seemed to water. Lovely, she was, my mother, and also Elise's, you know. Dead now. Well, then. Might as well say, as Father would say, if Father were younger and well again, the dew is on the grass again, the frost is on the windowpane. 'Come,' he would say, and then 'First of all and secondly'—the cries in the night. I tend to him—Father. Perhaps he would starve there or likely evaporate from thirst in the chair. He used to be ruddy, and red in the hands, as if his heart were in his hands. He built this house himself, for himself and for Mother. Mother sewed curtains. Night after night, we waited for word. 'First of all and secondly,' Father would say, and second counted more, of course. Mother stitched up hems again. Her vision was failing. She cured meat. Honeyed it. She sugared confections—better seen than eaten. Father spoke often of hunger and thirst, and of people, of children, and animals, lying in the road in the middle of the night or in the high heat of day, done in by their burden, or bodily need. Babies had perished, breathless and limp. Mother called Father by name on occasion. Listen, I heard this. Blood was on the floor in there. I'm telling you. Sweet—that was his name for her. Sweetness. Someone, of course, had to wash it away. There was nothing in writing. Mother's wrist was ruined then. I saw it. I washed it. Someone stitched it up in death. The thread did not match. And oh, such a woozy bundle of flowers, in bloom at the service. Rather unfortunately violent in color, if anyone there would have asked my opinion. All day long the noise of shoes—pumps in the vestibule, ladies, of course, dressed properly up; Elise, of course, absent. Somebody fainted from heat that day—or took a spell or suffered a seizure. Father took a drink or two. I also took a drink or two—our breath is not visible. I like to drink a bit at night. I tend to the glassware also at night, I rinse it: tumblers and glasses and cups and flutes and mugs and flasks and so forth and bottles. Some of it is crystal. I might miss a spot or two. Impossible not to. A glass might break. I've hurt myself alone at night. Elise took nothing, as far as I know. Why? Why not? Is there something I'm missing? There is ash about the floor again, choking the dust. I know how it accumulates. Ashes and spittle. Ash and tobacco. The whole house reeks. I am sorry to say it. Yes it does, in point of fact, in spite of my efforts. Who here will speak of it? Father? The dead? Not as if father and not as if the child, whatever she called him, maybe the name of the father of him, that lover of hers—Junior, the second, it's possible, isn't it?—not as if he, the child, objects to such a thing. Not he! Why, given wherever he came from—days, weeks, years from here, or even how old he is, or who it is he's talking to. Late in the night he is growing, I think, in the middle of the night, getting thinner and taller. He has taken to probing. 'Why?' he says. 'Why, why, why,' as if he were somebody else again, and him with a fever breaking and raging. Listen, now. I do my best. I tend to him. Sponge him. Feed him too, such as he eats. I'll spare you the details. Jam and such, rice and such, sugars and starches. I cannot eat, and yet I grow heavy. The child is given to licking his fingers, wiping his mouth with a doubled fist—never heard of a napkin. Coughs as if to clear his throat. Thirsty, he is. Well, obviously, I have given him a nip. There is not any juice in this house nor milk, not one last drop, I'll vouch for that, not even dried. Elise might have seen to that, mightn't she, now? She might have provided. All she left was clothes behind, the mess of them, ragged, afflicted with holes. I sew a bit. I do, you know. I miss her. There, I have said it. Father is raving. I try to keep up. I feed and I clean him. 'Auntie,' he says, and I am competent to answer. 'What is the reason?'

he used to say. 'Why? Why?' I try to smooth his brow, you know. The skin is so fragile. I cook a bit. I open a sack and boil the water. Not but bones, the both of them. I wash a bit. I sweep. I never could leave. I am tired. Tired. Listen to me. I serve them both, the both of them, Father, the child. I never could leave here, could I?" she said.

There was nobody there in the room with her.

Grooming

"WHY?" SAID THE child.

"Why what?" said the aunt.

"Why there were three little pigs?" said the child.

"For heaven's sake," the aunt said.

The child looked peeved, it seemed to her. His face was thinned, reduced, she thought, as if the fat of his cheeks had been consumed in the night.

"Why?" he said.

"When did *this* start—why? why? Who taught you that? Who talks to you?" the aunt said. "Other than me?"

"Me?"

"Who? Father?" the aunt said.

The child sat silent.

"Impossible," the aunt said.

"Stop it," the aunt said.

"Why there were three little pigs?" the child said.

"Auntie," the child said.

"I'm *hungry*," the child said.

The aunt said, "I don't doubt it."

"Why, why, why?" said the child.

"God," said the aunt. "If you are going to insist."

The child let a breath out. "Why?" he said.

"Suppose," she said. "God in his wisdom—his infinite wisdom—decided it fit to make three little pigs. Who knows?" she said. "Who is to say? Ours, as a certain person—who, for now, shall not be named—ought well to have taught you, ours is not to question."

The aunt took a sip, or rather, perhaps, to be blunt, a slug, from the tumbler at hand.

"I am tired," she said.

"Tired," he said.

"Sleepless," the aunt said. "Up all night. Not as if anyone else in this house would so much as notice.

"Eat," she said.

There was rice on the floor, and something else smeary.

"Eat, I said."

"I can't," he said. "Please."

"Swallow," the aunt said.

"How can I?" the aunt said.

"Say it," the child said. "Auntie, please. Once upon a time—"

"Once upon a time. The things I concede to," the aunt said. "See? But you already know it almost by heart."

"Pig," said the child.

"Yes," said the aunt. "The first little pig, to get to the crux, and the second little, you know, and likely as well"—she took another slug—"the peddler of sticks and the peddler of straw, hay, grass, old lily of the valley, whatever it was—dead."

"Dead?"

"Don't ask why, I haven't the patience."

"Why?" said the child.

The aunt's hand shook.

"Who talks to you?" the aunt said. "You know who you remind me of?"

The child scratched. The rash had scabbed, the aunt saw. The margins were ragged.

"Do you?" she said.

Dark liquid fell.

He ate, spilled.

"The waste," she said.

"Just don't," she said. "Don't tell me, then. Or is it you don't even know what I'm asking?"

"Big," said the child. "Big, bad."

The breath of the aunt seemed acrid to her, almost putrid, in fact, and hot to the tongue. She felt the urge to spit ("Resist" is what Mother would surely have told her, ever the afterthought after her death—the voice the aunt minded). She forced down saliva. "I'll get to that," the aunt said. "Give me a minute."

"Huff," said the child. "Big, bad."

"Wolf," she said.

"Huff," he said.

"Not yet," the aunt said. "Suppose for a moment the big, bad wolf was saving his breath."

"Why?" said the child.

"What do you think?" the aunt said. "He was not in a hurry. That is what *I* think. Yes, I do. Suppose, for the sake of discussion, the big, bad wolf had a perfectly adequate dwelling of his own. It's possible," the aunt said. "Entirely conceivable, isn't it, now? So here is the wolf at ease in his house, secure in his house, and, let us say, preening. The wolf, you see, is vain. He is, perhaps, installed in, as Mother would call it, the little girls'—the powder room. Oh! Can you hear him—whistling a tune? He is licking his chops. Perhaps he is shaving."

"Ssshh," said the child.

"Shaving," the aunt said. "Haven't you known a person to shave? Like so," she said. She touched her jaw—so dry this flesh! Injured. "The big, bad wolf was ever so slowly removing the stubble, deliberately. He was splitting the hairs of his chinny chin chin—nice and smooth and bloody clean."

"Clean?" said the child.

"Clean," said the aunt. "As if you would know. Except, I am sorry to say, this razor of his was somewhat corroded and, shall we say, dull."

"Dull?" he said.

"Dull," she said. "The wolf paid no heed to this."

The child appeared blank to her.

"The wolf had a fervent desire, you see, to be received as, let us say, civilized. Dapper, in fact. Not coarse," she said. "And so, despite an instrument of cutting that, now that I think of it, was dripping with blood—"

"Blood?" said the child.

"Blood," said the aunt. "A bloody blade, for God's sake."

A cough was heard from down the hall, a sharp hack.

"You see?" the aunt said. She swallowed a mouthful.

"Evil," the child said. "Burn, burn."

"Gracious," she said. She looked at the child. "Look at you. Just look at you. Who talks to you?"

"Huff," said the child. "Burn, burn."

The aunt, in order to stay her hands, steepled her fingers. Red, she saw—the knuckles—they were bruised, even purpled from washing.

"Wolf," he said.

"Lord," she said. "Forgive me."

"Why?" said the child.

She set her sights lower. "I have forgotten," the aunt said.

★ ★ ★

"Why?" said the child.

His face appeared thinner than ever to her, and sallower. He sucked his cheeks, the aunt saw.

"Why blood?" he said.

"Not this again. Ask me something else," she said. She fingered ice. She drank. "Listen," she said. "Why not ask, for instance, why she—that mother of yours—has up and gone?"

Father,
in a Rare Lucid Hour,
Speaks

"YOU," SAID FATHER, in motion in the chair. "You."

"You?" said the child.

"You," said Father. "We've spoken, you know."

"Why?" said the child.

"Come," said Father. "Here. Come close." Father reached forward as if, the aunt thought, from where she hid, he might, in fact, intend to kiss the child.

"Listen," said Father. (The aunt strained to hear.) "Knock, knock."

"Knock?" said the child.

The aunt drew back.

The child made a noise that sounded to the aunt like a weak engine revving.

"Wait," said Father. "Not so fast. You have to ask, 'Who's there?'"

Lovers and Angels

"WHO DOES SHE take me for?" she said. "Your mother. How could she? Listen. Just listen. My flesh and my blood."

"Blood?" he said.

"Don't," she said.

"Auntie?" he said.

The heat seemed to rise to her. She looked at the shelf where the bride—all net and artifice—had, all these many years, stood. "Gone," the aunt said. "Look."

Someone had taken her, broken or not.

"Mother," Elise said. "Help me now."

★   ★   ★

He had entered the bathroom.

The flowers were rancid.

"Smell," she said.

"Inhale," she said.

He sat down tubside, rubbed his jaw.

Her skin, sloughed off, lay afloat in the water. The water had darkened.

The stems were distorted with rot in her hand.

The lover said, "Well, then. Why did you take them?"

Elise said, "I hate it when you knock."

"The father pig, whose story, for reasons of history, remains untold, was given, quite likely," the aunt said, "to certain tenacious economies of speech."

The toes were shriveled, pink, she saw, and raw—as if new.

"Who is it?" the aunt said.

She rose in the water

"Knock, knock," the child said.

The aunt said, "You gave me a start."

The lover brought a knuckle to the side of her head. He said, "Is anybody home?"

★ ★ ★

It was dark in the house.

She dusted the shelf with the pads of her fingers for want of a rag.

She wrote in dust, erased.

Her palm held her fortune.

Here was the child, forever underfoot.

"Me?" he said.

"Up?" he said.

"Me, me, me," he said.

"Tell me," the aunt said. "Honestly. Listen. Your mother—she came here for this?"

The child was given to waking (or some kind of semblance of waking) in the night. He too, the aunt thought, this restlessness inherited. She'd heard the child murmur, in fever (and ever so slightly, of late, was there evidence of jaundice). "Coal" or "cold" the aunt heard, or "co" or "go"—or maybe it was something entirely different. "Huff," he'd said once, she thought, and "mama," and once he had wandered, in search, she imagined, of what he had come with: the white—or was it flax-haired?— doll.

★ ★ ★

"The mother pig should, by all rights, have died, rather peacefully, at ease," the aunt said, "with her pillow plumped properly up, in bed."

"Knock, knock," the child said.

"Who is there?" the aunt said. "As if I can't tell."

She covered her breasts as best she could. She drank from a cup on the lip of the tub.

"Now you may enter," the aunt said. "Come."

"No shame" is what the lover, retreating, had lastly asserted—yes? Or was it rather a lack of faith? She failed to remember. Night upon night—the spent clothes, soiled purse, faces in windows; a coin she had hidden like a fortune in a lining, lost. See how she conjures the dream of her life: Here is nothing from a hat, a city never visited—tents of sheets, as in a veritable fortress—iron from a well. Oh, drink! See such a trough as this! Unsoppable. The blood was on the bedding, and afterward the afterbirth. Boil the linen. Tear the skin. The boy had rent a place in her. The towels were ruined, the belly unfillable, save by blood, by risen heat. Reemptied, she wanders (to, fro), hair in the face, chinned hand. The breast is unsupportable. Limp is the child, and bloody to the touch; he is ablaze in the light. The train can be relied upon. Soap, mints, perfumes—none shall hide the scent of them, mother from child. She listens for something: a whistle, perhaps. She knows the child by smell, taste. Her knee holds a splinter. Who now shall witness: See how the body in blood is changed or rearranged or maybe transported.

Father, the aunt thought, to gauge by hand, mouth, lips, was dreaming of a cigarette, or maybe of affection.

The child said, "Auntie."

"Stolen," the aunt said. "Stolen from me. But this? Why this? Is it some kind of joke?"

The child held something tightly in hand.

"What is it?" she said.

"The house was not appropriate," the aunt said. "Ergo, the trouble."

"No," said Elise (a woman—imagine—who had always, as if in sleep, said "yes; yes, please; please, yes; a sliver, please, a drop"). She moved her head from side to side. The lover had been wrong in the particular of this: faith, shame. For she had fallen to her knees, wherever it was in the world she was, and in the night, in the dark, and with the child, had prayed.

Who Is There?

"KNOCK, KNOCK," the child said.

"Auntie?" the child said.

"Auntie? Auntie!"

The aunt was on her knees. She had her face in her hands.

"Oh," said the child. "Peekaboo?"

Part Three

THE RING

The Aunt's Dream

A MAN COMES to an inn. He is a robust fellow, of a type one often sees in such parts of the country. His cheeks are ruddy. His jaw is rather coarse and stubbled, as if his morning ablutions were insufficient to carry him through the day. It would appear that this fellow is a bachelor in early middle age, and of a moderate income. His attire is that of a merchant. The trousers are clearly not cut from high-quality fabric, and the topcoat, a dark, rough weave, shows flecks about the shoulders. The merchant arrives with a bored-looking servant, a haggard sort with putrid breath, thin dry hair, and a nose that gives evidence of having been broken. The servant walks with the limp one acquires in the course of a lifetime of service, when one has attained a certain age.

He leads the horses to the stable. He will see to the feeding and grooming of the beasts, and he will carry the tattered valises of the merchant up the flight of stairs and down along the length of the ill-lit corridor that leads to the room (like every other room) that, vacant, awaits. There he will lay out his master's various articles of toiletry (shave brush, razor, salve) as well as his garments. The room can be easily imagined, as rooms invariably are in such inns that cater to this sort of commerce: lacking adornment, indifferently swept, and with a narrow iron bed and with thin gray sheets and with a basin for washing. The basin is chipped. The ventilation is poor. The room will acquire the smell of its occupants. Insects scurry even in winter.

The merchant, having parted from his servant, enters the common room of the inn. A number of travelers of similar complexion sit in the green damask armchairs. They smoke. There is a bellows by the fire, a poker and a broom missing straw. The hearth is stone. The chairs, upon closer inspection, are pitted and discolored.

An inn servant enters through a dark kitchen door with a tray full of hot, bitter coffee in thin china cups with faded rims. He is a short, swarthy man who speaks a foreign language.

The merchant settles himself in a chair, not far from a window. He licks his lips. The proffered cup is spilling. He clears his throat repeatedly. Roads in this part of the country are dusty and seldom paved. He spits.

There is spittle on the floor. A woman, the innkeeper's

wife, perhaps, enters from the kitchen with a basket of bread, dark crusty loaves that are visible under a napkin; heat rises off them. Greasy broth with pallid scraps of meat or of cabbage, or barley, perhaps, will doubtless follow. The woman is fleshy and stout with a large double chin. She has covered her hair with a kerchief; her skin is scarred, and her apron strains about her belly and breasts. She does not speak.

The men speak of theft and of a pox and of looting. The merchant says, "Please."

The curtains are damask, faded, with some sort of intricate pattern of flowers. They are old and have been parted. The view is of the road. The leaves of a tree move in the wind.

The merchant desires that his room be made available. His belt is rather uncomfortably snug. He feels a pressure in the bowel. The coffee is acrid at the bottom of the cup, where grounds remain.

The merchant does not fall in with the discussion at hand. He is contemplating something. The fire appears to be unusually active. His stomach rumbles, but he makes no motion. Nothing is offered.

The men talk on. The stench is of smoke. The merchant's personal servant appears and is tugging at his elbow. The merchant is flushed. His gaze is directed, as ordered, implored, to what is outside the window: a carriage in flames.

A Particular Flower
with Astringent Qualities,
Often Used in Winter Bouquets

"AUNTIE," THE child said.

"Auntie!" the child said.

"Fire?" the aunt said. "Where?" she said. She rubbed her eyes. "Where am I? Where were we?"

The child stood to the side of the table on which the aunt had laid her head.

"Look," he said.

She tried to look. The side of her face—the flesh of a cheek—felt sore to her. Crumbs stuck to her, dried grains of rice; she felt them. Fluid was dripping. Her neck felt damp. "Where?" she said. "Tell me. You must tell me. Tell me where?"

"Look," he said. He stood in the bedroom, Mother's room, inside the dark sanctum, as if he belonged.

"Goodness," the aunt said. "What have you done?"

The child had something not his in his hand. The smell was familiar. Poison? She wondered. What was this? What he held was peau de soie.

"Where in the world did you get that?" she said (as if she did not know, she thought, appraising herself). "Why, you've given me a start. It was Mother's, you know. My mother's, you know."

"Mama?" he said.

"Mama?" he said. He raised his arms. He looked at her, pleading.

The bag simply dangled.

"Oh," she said. "Oh, no," she said. "You mustn't look at me like that. You know I'm not Mama, nothing of the sort."

"Why?" he said. He touched her wrist.

"Why blood?" he said.

"Listen," the aunt said. "Listen to me. The story is meant to be bloody, you know. A rule of thumb. Believe me. Even, you know, the third little pig, the third and supposedly good little pig, was guilty of murder. You know what that is?"

"What?" he said.

"Justification," the aunt said, "is never really innocence."

"Why?" he said.

"Just stop," she said. "Just give me that. Hand it." She snatched what the child held in his hands, had pressed to his cheek. "There, you see, Mother's—another of her pocketbooks." This one, the aunt saw, appeared to have been mended; it bulged.

"Want it," the child said.

"No," the aunt said.

"Mine," he said.

"Me," he said.

"No," she said.

"Why?" he said.

"See here," the aunt said. "Nothing is ours here."

Father was snoring again in the chair—she could hear it from here. "Tell me," the aunt said. "Where did you find it? Where was it kept?" She forced the clasp. She opened compartments, all but tore a seam. Ah, the aunt thought—mothballs. The poison of memory.

The bag was not empty.

Everything fell:

> Mints—inedible.
> Desiccated tissue.

Pins.

Hair.

A folded scrap—

"Auntie?" the child said.

"Quiet now," the aunt said. Her breathing was heady with chemical deterrent. She held the scrap of paper, unsteadily at best.

The child scratched. He looked to the aunt, the aunt thought, as if in search of rebuke, or any evidence of care.

The aunt directed herself instead to what appeared on the paper, undoubtedly drafted in Mother's hand:

Gloves (two pair)

Statice/Sea Lavender

Bows

Shears (to be sharpened)

Fix shoes

Something else was stricken out.

"Mama?" the child said.

"Ssshh," the aunt said.

"No," she said. "To whatever it is." She forced back the contents—oddly lumpy sack, this—and shut it, the whole pale thing, in a drawer.

"Statice," the aunt said. "Figure that. Not lily. Not lilac at all."

"All?" said the child.

"All," said the aunt. She raised her hand. "Where is my glass?"

His eyes were red, liquid.

She took a sip. "Come," she said. She made a lap. "Come sit," she said. "Sit here. I have a story for you."

"Auntie," the child said. He and the aunt were sated in the kitchen, not at the table, both on the floor. A chair was on its back. Morsels, half eaten, clung to his chin.

"Please," said the child.

"Auntie," he said, "tell me again."

"I can't," she said.

"Where?" he said.

"You know what I need is a bath," the aunt said. "Indeed."

That Which Elise Took

1. One small figurine—the bride, in fact, which had once adorned the cake, and which she, Elise, had previously accidentally broken, for reasons one can only presume were of overwhelming sentiment.

2. A letter, written by her, Elise, intended to remain in the house but inadvertently taken. This letter was shortly thereafter recovered by a gentleman, a merchant of sorts, who was riding the train and who, knowing nothing of its origins, tucked the thing into the space between the seats. The letter read as follows:

Dear A:
As you will see, I did not take much. I left what I had come for—that which I had come for—with you, in fact.

For you. You might come to need it. It is basted in the lining of Mother's silky clutch—you will know, I assume, which one I refer to. As for the child, you realize, of course, I am unable to take him. He has never known his father. The child's condition, which now appears to be graver in nature than I at first had dared to think, will pass, I pray, or be subdued. Please, if you will, put salve on the skin.

You will recall, doubtless, the way we were raised, with clothes on our backs and clean sheets on our bed. Two or three of everything. Mother once said that you were the one who was born of a passion, conceived of heat. Did you know she once spoke so frankly to me? I hear her voice again at night—Elise, Elise, Elise—and yet I cannot see her face, nor even envision, at times, my own. The child is named for his father, you know. I did try to tell him. He slept on the train. I would sing him to sleep, would lull him to sleep, would tell him Mother's stories, and Father's as well, though I doubt he understood much. Perhaps he was sleeping. I cannot account for the dream of my life.

Father will not last long like so. The day will come when others inhabit the place of our house. The furnishings as well, perhaps, will find some other use. The drawers will hold others' intimate garments, the beds a fresh impress. Even our voices will no longer echo.

Mother loathed these things of hers—the lamp, a gift that long ago, she told me, was worth a small fortune. Mother despised it. Broken now. Dark now. The silver is ruined. The jewel, she'd hidden in case she might need it. She told me herself. Chin up, she said. Remember that? You have grown so old with him—ancient!—and you not yet thirty. I lift my eyes and see my hands. I know what I have wrought of them. Believe me. The child, I take it, will feel me, will think he must see me, always, here and about, and, with the whistle of the train, will conjure my breath. "Go?" he used to say at night. Be gone, dark angels! This guilt I hold is also my hubris. Mine is the blood that flows in his marrow. All of our stories— Mother's, Father's—become his too.

Use it, dear sister—what I have left you—for what it is worth. We shall not meet again in life, but you remain in my heart for as long as the soul shall remain in the body.

—E

See No Evil

"KNOCK, KNOCK," the child said.

"Knock, *knock*," the child said.

He touched the stuffed arm. Father remained unbudgeably asleep.

"Knock, knock," the child said.

"Auntie," the child said.

"Stop there," the aunt said. "You mustn't ever enter when I am indisposed."

He looked at her.

"In the bath," the aunt said. "What I mean."

"Mean?"

"What did I say? I said *mustn't*," the aunt said.

"Why?" he said.

The water seemed to enter her; she felt the warmth seeping.

She lifted the washcloth ever so slightly.

"The body," she said.

"What is it?" the aunt said.

She thought—could have sworn, all but wagered her life—that she was smelling smoke again.

"Father," she said, "am I imagining this?"

"Huff, huff," the child said.

She felt the child's forehead. She brought her warmed hand to her less warm brow, gauging the difference.

"James," she said. "Jim," she said. "Baby?"

The breath of the child smelled to her of disease.

"Huff, *huff*," he said.

"Don't," the aunt said. She wrinkled her nose, as if for show, for someone else.

The aunt woke up, as was habit for her, in the dark of the house. She was waiting for it—the train; oh come, I said!— and stood by the window and yearned for reckless exile.

Even the curtains failed to move, this airless night. She held herself and felt the breath exit her body.

She covered her mouth.

"Huff," said the child.

"Not tonight," said the aunt.

"I said no," said the aunt. "And as long as we're on the topic of this, might it ever occur to anyone here that the third little pig defiled his house?"

"Eat," she said.

He swallowed.

She drank.

"Auntie," the child said.

"Knock, knock," the child said.

"Peekaboo," the child said. He stood there before her, sticky little hands of his blocking her sight.

"It's me still," the aunt said.

"Listen," the aunt said. She took his hands off her, held them a moment. "Eat, I said. There is nothing to drink in this house in terms of juice or milk or anything. Tonic, we're out of." She dripped.

"Here is a towel," the aunt said. "Cover yourself. Let me cover you now. There you go. Dry now. Clean."

The water had darkened.

Father coughed. He was unstable on his feet. He held the aunt below the arm where flesh hung loose.

The aunt drew back, away from the breath of him, the terrible sex of him, but dared not release him. Nevertheless, he was slipping from her, the flesh like rags. His ribs were large, and dark his eyes. Solid. Unmoving.

"Auntie," the child said. He stood in the doorway, toy—bedraggled thing—in hand.

"Wait," she said.

She said, "Where did you find it?"

Father, so guided, sat coughing atop the commode. His wetted clothes lay on the floor.

"Where?" she said.

The child came forward as if to make an answer.

"Wait," the aunt said. "Didn't I tell you? Cover them, cover your eyes."

A Man on the Train

SILVER COINS ELUDE his hand. He clears his throat. A city is moving unseen through a window. He reaches, in search of what was lost, between the seats, finds nothing, wrappers, stray pills, a folded-up message for somebody else. He rubs his jaw. ("Toothache?" she'd offered. "Bloody itch?")

"What was she thinking? Impossible," he says.

He rises and sits back down in his seat.

"No faith," he says, as if, thinks a woman sitting beside him, scolding himself. ("Shameless," he'd said.) He tries again and touches metal. Heat rises through him.

In another dwelling, unable to rest, he will sniff at the ink.

Coal

FATHER APPEARED TO the aunt in the night. The windowglow lit him, faintly, enough for the aunt to make him out. He had risen, of course, from the chair again. As if it were a shadow, she saw it: the smoke about the lips of him, issuing out of him; ashes, she thought, must fall to his feet.

"You," he said.

The aunt stopped.

She touched the wall. Both hands were empty.

"I wanted to save her." The voice, the aunt thought, had deepened in the night, as if it had been singed. Father had always been forceful of throat. Had he not stilled her, a child on his knee, his lap, or even his shoulders, held her there by dint of voice? *See this,* he'd tell her, the land he had fled from, bled in the dirt, abandoned belongings to lie in the road—cold gruel hardened; the children would perish again in his mouth, in Father's mouth, between his teeth, evoked as for sainthood or maybe perdition—lost, lost? And had she not heard him call out in the night in the wake of the train, and had she not trembled, listening, hidden: "Sweet," he'd said. "Oh, sweet," as if insisting, or begging, or crying for mercy? Father's voice consumed his chest. And had he not risen, not gathered himself to come to her, to speak to her, to question her, mercilessly, that merciless morning? Here was the question: *What did you see?* Elise had left—the first time. The question had echoed. And here Elise was, forever, it seemed, on the tip of her tongue, poised and indescribable. To say the gown had fluttered, the hair held the moonlight, witnessed thus: She, the aunt, unlovely sister standing there, dark in her nightdress— who would be served? Such a violent meekness! "Nothing," she, of course, had said when Father moved to question her. "Nothing, I said." And was it not given? Such was Father's grief in this, alone in the evening, Mother as if smitten, in the thrall of the unseen. She'd brought this on, abetted it, the aunt had, not knowing a person grew larger in absence. Would that she had cried out—but no, mustn't think that. Must not speak. (To think she would never hear Mother again, save from somewhere inside her, reconceived.)

Father's voice held her.

The body stammered.

The eyes, as seen by the glow from the window, were black, almost mineral. Combustible.

She, the aunt, met them.

"Go," he said. "Save yourself. Run, run, run for your life!"

One More Thing

FATHER HAD SOMETHING he'd found and burned, and once, perhaps once, maybe twice, had referred to. Slantingly written in Mother's hand, tucked into her bosom—pale this skin! lifeless—the note in its entirety read: "Girls."

Godspeed

AND SO THE aunt ran. Or, rather, in fact, to be precise, she moved with haste. For she was not well suited to run, grown heavy as she was, in gravity's bosom and not entirely easy in her gait, despite Mother's thoroughly rigorous teaching, coaxing, whatever you will—imperfect persuasion. Here the aunt was, underdressed; the hair unpinned or nearly so, the robe—which Mother, of course, had worn—pulled open on the aunt with the slightest exertion. Belt ends hung. The aunt was perspired again in the face. The night was warm, and she, the aunt, with some dispatch, as best she could, what with whatever assorted debris on the floor, what with whatever obstruction underfoot and with a certain fatigue that seemed impossible to budge, moved. She was winded already and still in the hallway, and blew out a breath. The walls seemed to move to her. She entered the pantry and found the light and turned it on, then off again; for rodents—if that, in fact, was what they were, presumably—went skittering. She left empty-handed. A taste was in her mouth.

She entered the bedroom in which the child lay and she went to the bed in which the child slept, and which, in fact, she herself, at one time, had slept in—a child—on occasion. The child was covered but only incompletely. The sheets, she suspected, were rather worse for wear, and even outright unsightly. Look at the child! He was thrashing in sleep and kicking in sleep and he was murmuring something— "co" or "go" she thought she heard—as if, she thought, he were speaking or telling a story to somebody dreamed of. "Mmmm," he said. Or maybe he said "morn," she thought, and "Mama." And so the aunt stood there and heavily breathed. He was shivering, the aunt felt; she touched his warm shoulder—the bones of him protuberant, alarmingly so—and she felt his warm chest where the flesh, she knew, was tattered and broken, and brought her hands up under him, beneath him, as if to surround him, and lifted him, hefted him—clumsy at first, for she had not yet held him, never this way, in this particular manner. Of course, she had groomed him and even, of course, had attempted to bathe him, to an extent, and more than once had brought him on her lap before bedtime to tell him a story, held him near, but never this—embracing the child, supporting his weight as he continued to sleep. To him she could be anyone. She breathed the child's breath. She staggered a bit, and held the child tightly, new in her arms, and heavy, surprisingly so—a strain to the back, to the arms—as if the body in sleep were impossibly dense. The aunt felt the heat of him enter her body, and swayed with the child for a moment thus. She had seen Elise do this. She smelled him, she did, sniffed him a moment as if to inhale him, the way the child smelled, of illness, she thought, and of flesh, and of rancorous teeth, and of unwashed hair, and of a memory of some rich milk. The aunt felt the body, its heat and arrangement, the almost molecular pull of it, as if her body must cleave to recollection of itself—how young she had been and where she had come from.

Still he slept, the child did, restless the eyelids, perceived more than seen, for the hallway was dark here, and lately, increasingly, the aunt's eyes failed her, such was her condition. She felt the child shivering. She turned on her heel, in a manner of speaking, reentered the bedroom and lay the child down on the sheet on which he'd lain—still warm and damp—and wrapped the sheet around the child and lifted him and stood there a moment and smelled him and listened to his breathing and laid the child down again, and, hesitating only a moment, removed her robe. She stood in her nightdress. Her body, it seemed to the aunt in the dark, was too exposed, in contour, if not completely in substance. The nightdress clung. She lay the child down on the robe on the bed, and she wrapped the robe around him—pallid

121

fleece that somehow, the aunt supposed, held something of Mother, a scent—and lifted him up again and brought her nose close to him. "Baby," she said. "My baby," she said, for there was no one to hear, save him, of course, and he, she thought, was listening in sleep to someone else.

"Mine," she said. She moved at night by what she knew, had known these years: the groove worn into the wood of a floor, a plank—loose—hard knobs, a bureau holding underthings, too-dark paintings, walls, the stippled concrete, lint that could all but be smelled in a cornice, a door she had opened in the dark. She moved with the child in her arms in the night, and her breathing was labored. She thought she heard Father and thought she smelled Father or Father's smoke, or maybe it was only that she thought about Father, and did not stop. She brought her feet in front of her and felt the wood amplified, hard against a weighty step, even in slippers—Mother's, of course, too tight, of course; they pinched her toes—never really truly hers. She forced the things off her, one foot freeing the other, and stumbled, almost. The nightdress continued to slip from a shoulder. She thought for a moment of searching for something, anything to pilfer—a jacket or wrap with a pocket or three—and thought to fill her hands again with anything of worth, such as silver or crystal, a coin that remained in the house unspent. Surely there was something here. But how was she to hold the child or put the child down again and pick the child up again—sleeping, of course; he slept, of course—and manage the burden? The child breathed. Elise had carried bags with her, paper, unsturdy, and brimming with whatnot, unmentionable articles Elise had left behind, but back then the child had toddled, awake. Alert. He had spoken to her, his newfound aunt. She looked at him asleep like this. For as long as she lived she would see it again, she told herself, the whole of it—this house she had lived in, the all-consuming bulk of it—towels and linens and starch and cups and lingerie, fur hats, topcoats, fine, chipped crystal, a drink she had not drunk. Crumbs in the pantry were not worth taking. Thirst rose within her, a terrible thirst, such as none she had known, a dry heat burning, and yet she did not stop nor drink, and yet she moved forward.

The child breathed, raspy.

She moved through the house to the room she had lain in, had paced in, had listened to Father in, the room with the window at which Elise had stood at night—a curtain left flapping, a hole in the world. The bed, the aunt knew, without having to look, was in a state of disarray; the linen had fallen and likely was stained. The mattress reprehensible. She moved with the child and felt the muscles in her back and all the vertebrae, the pull there, and undertook an accident. Deliberate or careless, what was the difference? Mother's lovely, frilly lamp, the aunt's fierce elbow. The porcelain shattered, the face of the lady, and still the aunt moved, and cut her foot. The child did not awaken. The window was open. She felt her foot wounded and made no sound (as was her wont, she might have said—why, cross her heart!). Her hand found a chair. Her foot found a leg. She dragged it, and using the not inconsiderable heft of her body, and holding the child, brought the chair to the window. The back of it was wood, and hard, and of another century. She brought herself, somehow, holding the child, his face to her neck, his breath to her skin, to stand atop the seat of it. Elise had been faster. Of course she had been! ("Girls!" said Mother, inflected in a way that she, the aunt, must hear at night and even, not infrequently, during the day. "Step delicately.") The house flashed before her as if it were a life: Mother, Sweet, in the pantry, and some sort of comfit—glazed, dried; a doily, ribbon, napkins, bows, arrangements of flowers even in the wintertime, and runners on the tabletops, and tucked away entirely and stowed in every quarter, possessions as one must have in a life full of purpose—books and such, and papers, billfolds and ledgers and documentation, closets full of outerwear, properly cared for, shoes to match, and—oh! again!—linens, the cloth and the paper that make for a household. Agents of hygiene were stocked in the cupboards. Shelves rose high throughout the house, the bride atop the uppermost. See! The house is in action. Mother is lathering up in the bath; Father, of course, is somewhere present, moving with some small child or two—piggyback or held by hand, or maybe simply motioned for. Silver in the pantry—the knives have been spit-shined. Cover your eyes and see them again.

The aunt felt air against her cheek. Her head was in the window frame, more out than in. The air was damp. It moved. She could cry out for Mother as loudly as she wanted. Cry out for all she had failed to hold on to: those who came unrecognized, and those who had dropped in the night to their knees, had clasped their hands as if for strength, or else, perhaps, to stop themselves. The house was not hers, nor the clothes on the body, nor blood on the sheet. Would that she had bled there! The child stirred. The aunt breathed. She leapt, or rather, fell from the window holding the child, still holding the child, and felt her breasts pushed into her, felt her breasts against her ribs, as if they were bound there, pressed by the child, and held him, and stumbled in the dirt there, and stood up, dirtied, and coughed. There was pain in her ankle, a roaring thirst. She moved as if unknowing. She felt her foot bleeding. She felt a heat behind her neck as if it were breath. "James," she said. "Oh"—and heard Elise's voice in this, Elise in her mouth now, inhabiting her—in bosom, muscle, heart, in arm. The aunt tried to run. The child moaned faintly—at least, the aunt thought so. Her feet reached the tracks. She had glass in her foot; she was certain of this, for she had felt it cutting into her. Her feet, of course, were bare, and they were flat and they were tender. Her ankle was swelling, it felt to the aunt, and hair fell loose. She was sweating in the night. She moved in the night and she was following the rails, past anything: houses, hovels, a shadow of a factory, trees that were barren, lost socks, a ravaged dog sprawled dead in the road, dirt, of course, loose earth, salt, crumbs, wolves baying with hunger. She felt the child slipping and tightened her hold, as if she could somehow surround him completely. Something was coming—she knew it, not yet sound but surely disturbance, far away or under her, beneath her feet, below the ground, and closer, yes, closer, a presence, vibrant, tinting the night as blood does water. Sound broke out. She ran at last, the aunt did, erupted, panting, into a run, not looking behind her, ashes in the mouth of her, and Father, presumably, somewhere in back of her, and Mother, of course, dear Mother, of course, and always Elise; and ragged, the aunt's breath, with all of them beside her and all of them in front of her, and in her ears a rush of sound—Come to me! Come, come and find me!— a howl in the marrow. Running, the aunt ascended the platform, there in the night as if nowhere on earth, holding the child, limp in her arms, a doll in her arms but with the faint breath of life. And she, the aunt, held him. He opened his eyes, for a moment bright, as if he quite saw her, as if he quite knew her, and closed his eyes, and visibly trembled, chin tipped back, the breath released, as if in ecstasy, the aunt thought, as if, in fact, in love.

Printed in the United States
By Bookmasters